PRAISE FOR *T*[illegible]

“*The Legend’s Daughter* i[illegible]tion of real people struggling with identity, with lo[illegible] time, rooted in the rugged and indifferent beauty of Idaho where each character finds his or her mirror in water, in stone, in place. David Kranes shows how our tenacious love of life can transform any situation, large or small, into alchemy. We are all living inside these raw and well-drawn pages.”

—Terry Tempest Williams, author of *When Women Were Birds*

“These Idaho stories are vintage David Kranes. He, more than any other writer, is the one whose work spurs me to reconsider what fiction can do. He uses language like a knife and the worlds in his stories come off the page at me. We haven’t seen this Idaho before. I’m thrilled to have these new stories, every one of them provocative, riveting, and robust.”

—Ron Carlson, author of *The Signal*

“In these times of human disconnection—from one another, from the places in which we live—*The Legend’s Daughter* lassoes us with the delicate tether of David Kranes’ multiple gifts and brings us home. He is a storyteller and an elegant craftsman, a teacher asking us to develop ‘an appetite for the impossible,’ to remember what truly matters.”

—Mary Sojourner, author of *Solace: Rituals of Loss and Desire*

“David Kranes has given us ten stories, entirely various, often splendid, sometimes hilarious, or heartbreaking, about contemporary settlers who migrate into hideout enclaves they find in the river valleys of central Idaho. They’re seeking varieties of emotional connection to nature and/or one another, and to sources of pride. Our luck in the West continues. We keep getting these terrific books.”

—William Kittredge, author of *Hole in the Sky*

First Torrey House Press Edition, May 2013

Published by Torrey House Press, LLC
P.O. Box 750196
Torrey, Utah 84775 U.S.A.
torreyhouse.com

International Standard Book Number: 978-1-937226-15-2
Library of Congress Control Number: 2012955569

Cover art by Connie Borup • connieborup.com
Cover design by Jeffrey Fuller, Shelfish • shelfish.weebly.com

The Legend's Daughter

Idaho Stories

By David Kranes

CONTENTS

WHERE I AM...WHERE I'VE BEEN

When Clifford asked Woods his plans for the last week in September, Woods asked what he meant. Clifford said he was hoping to fly west to Idaho and fish the Salmon above Stanley—would Woods join him? Clifford and Woods drafted for the same firm in Bethesda. They'd played racquetball.

Woods confessed an ignorance; he didn't fish. Clifford minimized it: he'd handle the arrangements, he said. Idaho, in late September, was beautiful; fly fishing was holding a stick in your hand in water and waving it. Woods hesitated, said yes. His children both were at boarding schools, his wife, Beth Ann, worked full-time for the Department of Energy. Their marriage seemed more like a kept toy than a quickened breath—a thing saved, out of sight, for its remembered pleasures. Woods told none of this to Clifford.

"I've got the equipment," Clifford said. "Waders, vests, flies, rods. Just bring yourself."

Woods asked where they'd stay.

Clifford said *camp*. "We'll camp." He had a Springbar, foam pads, Quallofil bags, cookware, backpacks. "It's near the road," he said. "It's not that far. From the highway. Just downstream and across from where we'll pull in and park. Pines! It's beautiful! But civilization's..." He grinned. "It's 'in the wings,' so to speak. But don't worry. We can drive to Stanley, at night, for... whatever. You enjoy whatever? 'R & R,' is that what you call it?"

Woods told Beth Ann.

"Outdoors?" she said.

"Yes," Woods said. "Apparently."

She laughed, then stopped herself, pressed her lips tight.

"What?" Woods said.

"Nothing," she said. "I don't know. It's just, I suppose, interesting." She suppressed something. Mirth.

"What's interesting?" Woods said.

"They say Idaho's lovely," Beth Ann said. "September. Probably always."

Did other people, Woods wondered, talk like this? Seventeen years into marriage?

"It might be the start of something," Beth Ann said. "So... and that would be good."

"What?" Woods said. "Start of what? What...*good*."

"I can't—" she laughed, then stopped herself again. "Whatever," she said. "Whatever. What would you like?"

"Possibly," Woods said. He didn't know what he could add. He didn't know, really, what he had said. He thought how much he liked the gold earrings she'd begun to wear. He thought how nice she looked in quieter prints. He wondered: might she begin wearing her hair just a little longer?

Clifford assured Woods. "Just bring dry clothes," he said. "And money." He laughed. They flew from Dulles on September 12, Dulles to Stapleton, Denver to Sun Valley, where they rented a lipstick-colored Fieri.

It was late afternoon. At Silver Creek Outfitters, they bought flies, leader, something called *tippet* in different numbers, something called *gink*. The gink was a silicone gel, which, Clifford said, kept the flies dry; it came in a tiny, plastic dispenser. Clifford had gotten them a unit at a place called The Cobblewood. They went there and unloaded, then drove to where a local road crossed the Wood River and the water smoothed and slowed. There, Clifford gave Woods his first lesson: rod, three basic flies—Adams, caddis and grasshopper—knot-tying, gink-applying, and casting.

An hour later, in the long, balloon-shaped shadows, Woods had a trout. His line bent. He felt the pull, the fight, the strain.

Clifford talked gently and eased him through the play, the retrieval—all ritual—the netting and the release. It was exciting; Woods' heart raced. He'd never stood in the middle of water before. The casting was like a fine line-drawing. Like a rendering he might make. A draft. A sketch. Another fish took his caddis! And a third! The day's diminishing light spilled off and into the pasture grass and shrubbery. In the near-dark, yet another trout—Woods could feel its weight—took his fly with a jolt he'd not known. Woods drew in too hard; the line snapped, its filament taut and then weightless somewhere in the dark air. He wished Beth Ann could see. If she saw, she might find him different. Glimpse a quiet heat. A fire. She wouldn't believe she was seeing who she was seeing.

Smelling like the cold, in part like metal, in part like water, Clifford and Woods drove from the river and had Mexican food. The place was called Angelita's and the tables were unsteady; Woods kept spilling his margarita, losing the salsa off his blue corn chips. He felt energized, sexual, very hungry. Aware of his body. He'd grown up in Philadelphia, then lived eight years in New York before moving to Bethesda. It was almost frightening, the kind of pulse he was feeling at his wrist and at the back of his neck—the spill, the delicious snaking of...*what*? Something animal—loose aggression.

They ate what the menu called *carnitas*, and Clifford, non-stop, talked books. Woods had seen him alone in various cafés at lunchtime, jaw tight, reading, leafing pages. He'd seen Clifford head off into the men's room with hardbacks. Some of the names Clifford spoke Woods recognized—Hemingway; Pound; Stegner; the Russian, Turgenev. But there were others which just made sounds: Bud Guthrie, John Muir, Frank Waters, Van Tilberg Clark, someone named Parkinson, another...Turner; Boorstein, Kitteridge, Berry, Huizinga. An Indian, Black Elk. It was wonderful to watch Clifford's face while he rambled.

Clifford's notion, as much as Woods could follow, was submission. "We lose submission," he said. "Where we are in our work. Back. Bethesda. East. Drafting. We stop giving over. Giving in. We stop obeying."

It sounded wonderful—whatever Clifford said, the way he said it. He talked with his mouth full and with animation. There were smears of avocado on both his cheeks, dab of salsa on his forehead. He looked like a warrior. *Could I be a warrior?* Woods wondered. He thought maybe. He thought not.

Then Clifford's words turned to women: *phenomenal,* he kept saying. *Phenomenal*: how *phenomenal* women were. He was grandly drunk. "I don't mean vernacular phenomenal," Clifford said. "No. No-no-no!" He wrinkled his nose. "I mean, did you ever see a stone, say, in a streambed? Looks like something alive? Like a living thing? Actual living thing? All smooth? Veined? Embedded, kind of? With other minerals? That's what I'm talking about. Women. That's the thing I'm... like a miniature...what? Kidney, say, or aorta or something."

Woods ordered another margarita and nodded. Clifford kept spitting his food as he talked, but Woods didn't mind. He considered spitting his, too. It looked like fun.

Clifford had been married twice. "I can't get it right," he said. "I can't get it *close*, as a matter of fact. It pisses me. I want, but I can't. I'm too anxious. Or too. . .not anxious enough, possibly. Not alert. I read one thing when I should be reading another. I fall in love with a woman's neck, it should be her fingers. You know? I buy her Nanci Griffith, should be Reba McEntire. It's bad. Doomed. I talk when I should be quiet, I'm quiet when I should talk. I don't read the wind picking up. I'm talking figuratively, of course, but I don't watch the surfaces. Still, you've got to keep, I don't know, coming back, don't you think? *I* do. 'Come back, Clifford!' I say to myself. You've got to keep coming back. Know what I'm saying? I'm just saying, I would like to meet a woman—listen, hear this, Woods—pay attention—I would like to meet a woman, and I would like to feel that I was this *old man* who had known her—Jesus, I suppose forever—okay? All right?"

"That would be great," Woods said. He laughed. He couldn't stop himself. In the light and angle where he sat, Clifford looked like Beth Ann. The laughing seemed something that had been too long in coming. A source, a spring, that he'd not acknowledged in himself. An opening. A beginning.

Clifford slept like a corpse. Woods kept waking to the fresh air in their condominium and being stunned: ready to eat again, ready for some activity. He'd wake and leave his bed and walk into the living area and stand by the screen where the night air came in and listen to the sounds and wonder why he'd never come to such a place. Once he lay out, naked, on the Navajo rug and stared up at the unit's exposed beaming, where he swore he saw, through what he took to be chinks, the stars, the constellations. Comets, even.

In the morning, Clifford was reading when Woods finally woke. He seemed absorbed, immensely sober, almost shy. Woods made coffee, found packages of quick oatmeal with apple slices, made them. He felt a stranger to Clifford, where, the night before, he'd felt deep exhilaration to be such a friend. Woods set the table, conscious, with each silverware's contact, he was making sound. Clifford read through most of breakfast: a book on John Wesley Powell. Suddenly, Clifford stopped—slapped the book shut and barked: "New day! New day!"

Before they left, Woods called Beth Ann, at work, at the Energy Department, to say he'd arrived safely and had a great first afternoon. "I felt so happy," he said.

"Good," she said. "That was destined to start."

Her words confused him. Destined what? Start where? When he asked for news, she said she and her friend Daria had bought a house on the Chesapeake. Three acres. Ten rooms.

Woods, again, was unclear. "What do you mean?" he asked.

"I mean as an investment," Beth Ann said. "We both had money. It was underpriced—Daria knew the owner. It's a good area."

"My wife bought a house with another woman," Woods said as the two drove up and over Galena Summit. "Another woman," he repeated.

"Yeah, right. Women and other women," Clifford said. "They'll give up the short stuff all afternoon and then it's like *whoom*, Mystic Pizza or something!"

Woods furrowed his brow. He nodded. "I suppose," he said. He considered. Daria was thirty-five, married to a lobbyist. What, exactly, was his calculation? *A house on the Chesapeake. Three acres. Ten rooms. Why*?

To the west, the Sawtooths peaked and took Woods' breath away. They made the unmarred blue of the sky savage, inverted, ferocious. "I've never seen anything like this," Woods told Clifford.

"It's just the start," Clifford said.

They stopped for coffee at a log café in Stanley. Clifford pulled out his book, made no conversation. He turned a page—Woods clocked—every fourteen seconds. Had Beth Ann meant she and Daria were going to *live* in their house? They were going to *move* there?

Woods conjured an image: a room with bay windows, oriental rugs, wide floorboards, antique furniture, Telemann or something playing, late afternoon light, lawns sloping, riverfront, Beth Ann and Daria drinking jewel-red apéritifs out of two long stem glasses, heads thrown back, necks exposed, laughing. The teasing sense he'd had—just the night before—of giddiness, latent combustion, began to fade. He stood, walked to the postcards, chose one. It showed the Sawtooths behind an azure blot and was captioned *Hell Roaring Lake*. Woods addressed the card to Beth Ann, then wrote, "Where I am" in the message box. He bought a stamp. The café had a mail slot. He dropped the card in.

As they drove north from Stanley, the Salmon was beautiful: blue and turquoise, white with light and water. It snaked. It dropped into pools. Mid-range and miniature figures wearing waders and vests appeared and disappeared, hunched and poised, playing fish. There were great black and white scissor-tailed birds, jays with pitch crests, once what Clifford called a blue heron, beating its wings lazily, low, following the river.

"This is extraordinary," Woods said.

"The River of No Return!" Clifford announced.

They drove eighteen miles before Clifford slowed, maneuvered, and backed down into a dirt turnoff. "Ready for this?" he asked.

"I don't know," Woods said.

Clifford had everything, all their equipment. It was either in or strapped artfully to backpacks. "Boots, waders, and vests first," Clifford said. Woods prepared himself, watching Clifford, mimicking what went where, which socks over what; what the lacing, where the wader belt, when the vest. Then, when they were ready, Clifford helped Woods with his pack, grey canvas on a metal frame. Woods held Clifford's, which was larger. Clifford gave Woods a set of car keys, saying he had two: one zipped into the back pocket of his vest, another in his pants pocket. "Just trying to make sure we get out," he said.

The task was to cross the river, just downstream of where they'd parked. Clifford had given them both telescoping sticks, and before they set in, he reviewed what to do if Woods should lose footing: get onto his back, feet downstream, wait for the slower water. "We've got all day," Clifford said. "Don't tighten up. On the other hand, it's just a walk. Like any walk. It's just water. Try to take each step. I'll go first."

Clifford did. He moved out from the shore where the

water was slow. He had explained that he'd chosen this particular spot to cross because the river was wider. "It just *looks* faster," he said, "because you get more churn, but it's actually slower."

Clifford moved easily. "It's fine," he called back. "It's wonderful!" Woods entered. He moved in. Water slid by, and there was the sense both of motion and none. Still, it felt comfortable; there was a rippling at his calves, the way the Wood River had rippled the previous day. He followed Clifford at a slight distance. He liked the way the water jostled. "Why would a woman buy a house with another woman?" he called ahead to Clifford.

"Why are there cannibals?" Clifford called back. He laughed, then immediately answered his own question. "To get to the other side!" he said.

The other side?

Mid-river, the water rose to Woods' knees, and the weight of his pack seemed, suddenly, to pull him backwards. He lost his footing, then righted himself.

"You okay?" Clifford called. "I heard splashing."

"I think so," Woods said.

"Keep a base!" Clifford called. "Try to always keep a base under you. Triangulate. Don't walk frightened."

What did Clifford mean, "Triangulate?" What did he mean, "Don't walk frightened?"

They made the crossing. It seemed tricky, briefly, in the deeper flow; then, immediately, graceful, a glissade, fine. On the far side, there was a path trampled downriver until it opened into a pine clearing. "Ta-da!" Clifford sang. The pines were high. The clearing was small and vaulted, like a protected room—the river just beyond: not visible, but alive always, and musical. Birds called from high branches, and the pines, both above and underfoot, their mulch of fallen needles, made the place like an analgesic.

Camp was simple. Woods followed Clifford's lead, and, within half an hour, they had their tent up, food cached, fire arranged, a small table structure contrived. "Home!" Clifford said.

"Home," Woods tried to repeat, but the word snaked him, his upper spine, like a bare wire, a small power surge. "Home almost," Woods said, qualifying. Instead of their camp, he imagined a ten-room house. Words with *W*s came in: *wolverine, women, water.* He tried to smile, and they headed for the river.

Clifford was incredibly mindful. "Drop your fly just in back of that rock where the water *V*s." Woods did. On his third cast, a huge rainbow hit just as the fly was drifting past the rock. "Jesus!" Woods said. He got too excited; he reacted too fast and lost the trout. "You want it too much," Clifford advised, in a voice so low and modulated that it was eerie.

"What do you mean?" Woods asked.

Clifford said nothing.

Clifford pointed to the edges of riffles. He pointed to weedy overhangs along the bank. Woods felt himself Clifford's friend. Clifford would talk him through each netting and release. Once, when Woods stepped into the current to a depth threatening to spin him—the water ripping hard around his thighs—Clifford eased out and extended a stick and talked Woods back.

In the late afternoon, sun just above the trees, Clifford asked Woods if he would be all right on his own a while; he said he was going to work the river down and then upstream by himself, then they could think about quitting. Woods said he'd be fine. He watched Clifford pumping his arm in a steady rhythm, left then right: solid, relaxed, at home. He saw a fish larger than what they had been catching rise to what Clifford had called a "humpy," and then watched the fish and Clifford play each other in a kind of dance until Clifford coaxed the fish into his net. "Great!" Woods called down the length of water. But if Clifford heard, he didn't turn; he didn't respond.

When Clifford disappeared, Woods suddenly felt vulnerable. And alone. It wasn't the water. It wasn't a feeling that he might again stride out of his depth and be swept away by an element he couldn't measure and didn't understand. That prospect—truth told—beguiled him, felt hypnotic. It was that the man had been so good. Clifford. It was that the man had been so caring. All day. And had been so patient. It was that Woods felt embraced. And wondered why this strange, eccentric man—at one minute, bookish, the next, manic—had invited him to travel so far from Bethesda.

Woods felt himself well up. He began to cry. The light diminishing, he stood thigh-deep in a quiet eddy and a flood of tears. He felt loved by...*what*? Something, the world, and confused in that. He felt attached. Yet—

Yet there were all these images: images of Beth Ann that kept coming in. Beth Ann and Daria. The two in some small café. Or at a concert. And their two faces were like twins: so alike, so satisfied, composed. What was he seeing? Were his and Clifford's faces alike? A trout struck his fly where he had allowed it, downstream, to drift, unattended. He played the fish. Brought it in. Clifford's voice spoke in his head, coaching. In his net the fish looked like the infant he and Beth Ann had lost, after Clark and after Michelle, in the hospital. Woods released himself to an almost trumpeted sobbing. The water grew dark, then darker; the light just a filtering weight in the trees.

When Clifford reappeared, it was along the path. In his hand was a green tackle box. "Treasures!" he called. Woods moved out of the river to join him.

In the box were cosmetics: lipsticks, powders, brushes, creams, eyeshadows and liners, blush. Clifford speculated a household where the wife, because the case was large and traveled easily, had taken one of her husband's tackle boxes for makeup, and that the husband, bolting for Idaho, had grabbed the appropriated box and, when he found out, had been infuriated and had left it beside the river. What other explanation? "I'll bring it home for my next wife!" Clifford said. "Who knows? It might prove a bargaining chip."

At the campsite, Clifford lit a halogen lamp, pulled a bottle of Maker's Mark from his pack, poured for Woods, and made a fire. All the while, he spoke with animation: asking if the fish seemed different to Woods at dusk and which flies he'd used. Set off, perhaps, by the tackle box, Clifford talked more about women. He said that, once, a girlfriend had left him in her apartment while she went out for clotted cream, and he had just, as an experiment, shut his eyes and drifted through her rooms, his instincts in charge. "I ended up in her closet," he told Woods. "Between a camelhair suit and a silk dress! And then I had this crazy idea and I *did* it. I opened one of her… scents, I guess they call them, this thing called "Diva." And I poured a shot glass. And drank it. Got really sick. I was on the floor when she got back. She called a cab and got me over to Holy Cross. They pumped my stomach. It was wild. But—I have to say, even though I couldn't tell you—it was worth it. It was a trip."

Clifford finished his tale, then disappeared quickly into the dark and toward the river. Woods watched. He drank, tugged his whiskey, its taste curiously less musk and more florid. Still—there in the dark and fish-tasting air, cold and liquid and flickering with lamp light—it tasted better than any whiskey he could ever recall.

When Clifford sauntered back, he retrieved a book and began reading. He read for two hours, while Woods sipped whiskey and grew hungry. The book was a book Woods hadn't seen: something about the Cree Indians. Woods wondered what the dinner plans were. He heard bird and insect and animal sounds he had never heard before. He wondered: were sounds like this the lure of the Chesapeake? On impulse, he opened the green tackle box and rummaged, rearranged all its tubes and small jars and brushes. Whoever the woman had been, she'd glued a cheap mirror to the inside lid, and Woods tried to see himself. But the mirror coating was a thin silver and blotched any image with a thick and arterial branching.

About nine, Clifford slapped his book shut and beamed. "You didn't bring reading?" he half-asked, half-chastised Woods.

"I should have," Woods said.

"You always should have," Clifford grinned. "You always should have! You always should have!" He made a litany of the words, then poured himself whiskey and drank it straight. "Life is one continuous motion," he said, and Woods thought he understood.

Within twenty minutes, Clifford had made pasta, and the two ate and sipped more whiskey. "Tomorrow night, we'll go into Stanley," Clifford said. "I'll take you to the whorehouse."

Woods flinched.

"I'm just kidding," Clifford said. "I *think* I'm just kidding. I *may* be just kidding. If I'm not kidding, I don't know about it yet." He laughed. "It's a *male* whorehouse."

Woods lay awake for several hours in their tent, listening. It was as if the river were percolating, just beyond, out of the rocks. He had never done military service and wondered whether this, in any way, was like that, like the life of a soldier. He fantasized Beth Ann and Daria just beyond his tent, outside, by the fire's embers, sitting watch. Women became friends—wasn't that right?—more easily, more frequently, than men. Were he and Clifford friends? Were they becoming friends? How could Woods tell? How could he determine that?

In the morning, Clifford made them cheese omelets and

biscuits, brewed fresh coffee. Cooking seemed matter-of-fact to him. The meal was delicious. "You do the dishes," Clifford said, tossing a scrub pad. He read while Woods fetched river water, boiled it, used it to wash and rinse the aluminum-ware. Woods finished and sat awkwardly to the side until Clifford looked up and said, "Listen: don't let me keep you," and went back to his book. Woods geared up and crossed to the river.

An hour later, Clifford joined him, and they fished all day—much as they'd fished previously. Clifford stayed near, gave tips. He produced sandwiches from his pack when the sun bore direct from overhead, dry fruit, two cold beers from where he'd stashed them in a pool of rocks. They sat in the shade, and Clifford asked Woods, "What do you most regret doing with a woman?"

Woods said it was more *not* doing, and he told some stories. "Three different women have told me that I seemed scared of them," Woods confessed. Clifford listened. He poured cold beer onto the crest of his head and massaged it into his scalp.

"I drove a woman to the airport once," Clifford said. "As if I were, of course, going to be there to pick her up when she flew back, although I knew I wasn't." He ground his teeth, shook his head. "I just sent her into the skies! Plural! Skies! I just sent her up." He spit something to the ground, some piece of dry apricot, and kicked dust on it. "We're not truthful—you know?" he said. "We're not a truthful species."

In the afternoon, they walked about a mile and a half downstream, and fished from a sandbar. Again, when the long shadows came, Clifford excused himself and slipped beyond a bend, leaving Woods. Again Woods felt lonely. And overcome. And vulnerable. Even abandoned. His heart raced and he felt almost feverish. He slapped cold river water to his face repeatedly to slow his pulse. Clifford reappeared by a far bank, intent, his rod arching. The biggest trout Woods had seen broke the water. Twice. Clifford played him, eased him in, seemed incredibly gentle, massaged the trout in the water, let him go.

They left the stream before dark. Clifford shaved; Woods followed; each used the tackle box mirror. They slipped on their boots and waders, no vests, and forded the stream. Clifford strung nylon cord, pine to pine, from the far to near banks. "We'll need this when we come back in the dark," he said. They drove the highway to Stanley, where Clifford took them to a roadhouse called The Joker. They drank whiskey and ate steak and watched some innings of baseball on the bar television. There was a small country-western trio playing, and two younger women at the bar. The women were raven-haired and asked Woods and Clifford if they'd care to dance.

So they did. The one with Woods, Karmine, nestling almost brutally into his shoulder. She wore a short, Denver Broncos cut-off jersey, exposing her midriff, and, at one point, asked Woods to unbutton his flannel shirt, which he fumbled with at first but did. She said she liked dancing skin to skin. It made Woods sad and dizzy and frightened. The adhesive stick and peel of their abdomens scrambled him. *Heat*, he thought. *Heat*. Had he lost heat in his life? Would these women want to "go home"?

Woods tried to make conversation, but Karmine said, "I don't like to talk." Across the dance floor, Rhonda, the other, and Clifford tangled and regaled each other, burst after burst.

"Thank you, ladies!" Clifford finally said. "We'd stay, but tomorrow's a school day, and my son has to get home." Rhonda laughed. Karmine looked at Rhonda, as if expecting Rhonda to take some next step, say something—which never got taken or said.

There was spilled moonlight on the river, and Clifford led Woods across, guided by the rope. Clifford sang "Amarillo by Morning" and invited Woods to join. Woods tried but didn't know the words. "Fake it! Fake it, for Chrissakes!" Clifford sounded enraged, then laughed, then lurched again into the singing: "Amarillo by morning...Amarillo…I'll be there!" Around them, the river roiled, thick as petroleum and gold-veined, seeming deeper than both knew it was.

Woods, at first, couldn't sleep. His system seemed over-stoked. Hypervigilant. Then he slept too hard, dreamt too urgently: dreams in which he could find no sensation in his legs and feet. He'd be loosed, in thick and cold water, circling, swept, and try to kick against a bed or hunching rock, but the message wouldn't fire; his brain couldn't locate his legs; his legs, the streambed. And there were dreams of large women who spent him, terror their sole arousal. He woke shaking and left the tent, dragging his bag, stumbling the path to the river, where he found a flat, open space in the long, matted grass and, exhausted, slept. In a new dream, his wife, Beth Ann, nursed him indulgently from a blue plastic bottle with a straw.

"Were you concerned?" he asked Clifford, returning, the next morning.

"Just a minute," Clifford said. "I need to finish this chapter."

They spent the day, again, on the water. A ritual had developed: Clifford coaching and instructing; Woods in digression. Clifford had undone the line they'd used to cross the previous night, "so as not to garrote some rafter." Woods confided his dreams; he confessed his fears that Beth Ann might have a life beyond him with another woman. "Buying houses," he said. "Having secrets."

Clifford laughed. "Secrets! Of course!" he said. "What do you want: of course she does!" He told a story about a woman, "Glorious Pasta," he'd met at the Atlanta International Airport. The woman had weighed close to three hundred pounds. They'd taken a room for two hours at the airport Hilton. She'd gotten his phone number, and for over two years, she would call and name a new airport. At first the airports were domestic; then, international. Clifford and Glorious Pasta made love in over forty airport hotels, and, by the end, she'd slimmed to a hundred and ten. "They use us for practice!" Clifford said. "We're only practice! They—I'm serious about this—warm up on us—but who can blame them?"

Woods nodded. Clifford pointed to some riffles. "Cast," he said. "Hit the slick water just before the churn." Woods did. An enormous cutthroat broke the surface, striking Woods' fly. He set the hook. "Perfect!" Clifford said. He talked Woods through the play and netting. It took half an hour. Woods was exhausted. The trout measured twenty-two inches. The two massaged the trout's white, glorious underbelly and set him loose. Woods burst into tears, wracks and surges which wouldn't quiet. "Good man," Clifford said to him. "Good man." And he kissed the crown of Woods' fishing cap.

Again, Clifford had prepared a lunch: brie cheese, fruit, sardines, dark ale. (Where did he get all this food?) He read a biography of Frederic Remington, while Woods squeezed lemon onto the brie and sardines set on crackers. Clifford told Woods that Remington's wife had changed his tombstone inscription. He'd wanted 'He Knew The Horse,' but she wouldn't be buried next to a man whose stone said that. "Interesting," Woods said, though he didn't understand why that single fact seemed so worth Clifford's announcement.

Again, they fished together after lunch. Again, Clifford slid off mid-afternoon by himself, diminishing then vanishing around a bend. Again, Woods felt alone: reduced, meager, divested of love, sexless. Both banks of the Salmon seemed painfully distant. No trout took his fly. He changed it. He changed it. When a fingerling rose and hit his Adams, it almost annoyed him. Woods was glad it was their last day. He thought, *I've gone far enough*, and the phrase stuck in his head, because he didn't really understand it. *I've gone far enough toward what*, he thought. *Toward where?*

Again, when the shadows grew long, grew weighted, Clifford returned along the far bank, working the grassy overhangs, trout rising on nearly every cast. Woods watched. Clifford was so intent, so detached from the world in which Woods, daily, knew him—a man unfixed by demands, modal like water. Closer, Woods could see Clifford pumping and pumping his arm, casting; hear him laughing to himself. His friend was not stable, Woods thought.

Both shaved in the cosmetics mirror. Both put on fresh clothes. Woods doused his face with cologne. Again, in their waders and boots, they crossed the river to the car, and again Clifford stretched and tied off the rope so that they could cross back in the dark on return.

Again, at The Joker, they drank whiskey and ate meat; the night's special was lamb chops, which came with fettuccini and salad. The club was busier: families, couples; mostly, though, it was men with men, women with women. Karmine and Rhonda entered at one point, spotted Woods and Clifford, strode to their table. Rhonda kissed Clifford on his cheek; it was a wet kiss. She grabbed his leg and laughed. "We may be in later," she said. Karmine stood by. She spoke no words, made no gesture. Then they turned and left.

Woods felt strangely disappointed. He wove his way to the men's room and peed. He thought about Beth Ann. He checked himself in the mirror and found Daria's face fixed where his face should be. How much had he had to drink? Then he was himself again—older, yet younger. The baked coloring of the three days on the water had brought out, in a kind of curious glaze, the young man he'd once been. But the heat had cracked his face as well, dug all the lines deeper. It was the death mask of a boy, and it shook Woods.

He left the men's room and couldn't find Clifford. Then he saw him: alone, gliding on the dance floor, arms wrapped around his own blunt frame, unashamed, in the most tender and clownish gesture. Clifford had his eyes shut. He was dancing cheek-to-cheek with himself. Two women danced, as well, apart, one with the other. They were the only others in the blue and smoky lights.

Woods phoned Bethesda. It would be past midnight. He didn't care. There was no answer. Not even his machine kicked in. It made him angry. It seemed unfair: he should at least get his machine. He fantasized a conversation:

Okay! What's going on?

Where, Woods?

Between you and Daria!

Whatever. Whatever—it's our business.

Then Woods fantasized lashing out. He imagined striking. He imagined Beth Ann's eyes glazing, her teeth tight and cruel. He imagined smashing every lamp in their living room, Beth Ann saying, *Who? Who do you think you are? You're pathetic!*

He ordered a whiskey. He threw it down, ordered again. Clifford was still in his moving trance: complete, content, in another place. No one in the bar seemed to register Clifford; it was as though his embrace of himself was common. Woods ordered a third whiskey and walked outside. Two bodies coupled under a blanket in the back of a Dodge pickup. The raven air wove the scent of broken stone. The couple under the blanket snorted and laughed. Woods felt mocked.

Inside, Clifford was paying their bill. Woods had offered to pay, but Clifford only sang, "On the road again..."

On their drive to the river, Clifford was ababble—relentless—about "mirror souls" and "mirror universes." It was all a rank stupidity to Woods. Woods was tired. He was upset. He was probably drunk.

They parked. The moon, in and out of clouds, burned the river like black metal, then lost itself to clouds, like ashes. "How much did you drink?" Clifford asked. "Not enough," Woods said. He tumbled out of the Fieri, then got to his feet.

Clifford geared himself, then coached Woods into gear—boots, waders. He suggested Woods try to vomit. Woods did. The whole night, it seemed, came up. Clifford held him. He massaged Woods' shoulders and his neck. Woods' eyes felt aboil. "That's good, guy, good," Clifford kept saying. "Get it out." Woods' breath came in heaves and throes—fast, sudden; still, he felt better. "Okay," Clifford said. "Okay, splendid."

Clifford propped Woods against the car and set off to find the rope. Woods heard him say *shit, fuck!* And then *piss! God-damn!* in the darkness. Silence, then Woods heard, *saw*, Clifford trudging back. Clifford didn't look happy.

"Some asshole!" Clifford said.

"What?" Woods said.

"Cut the rope," Clifford said.

"So, what? What?" Woods couldn't put it—whatever Clifford was implying—together.

"Listen," Clifford said. He slipped an arm around Woods, encouraging. "Listen: what we'll do is, I cross. Okay? I've got another rope—always bring rope. I'll cross back. We tie it off. We both cross back together. All right?"

What was Clifford saying? Woods couldn't figure.

Clifford played himself back. "So, then: *you*…you stay here," he finished. "Okay? You stay here. I know the river. I'll be quick." The moon broke, almost blinding, then was lost. Clifford eased Woods down. He did something at his back, where his suspenders were. "Listen," he said. "Sit. I'm going to sing the whole way. You listen to my voice. If I hit one false note—okay? Going over, crossing back—I owe you a hundred bucks. So, listen! Don't miss this! It's an opportunity!" And then Clifford did what he'd done once before: kissed Woods on the crown of his head.

"Ribbon of darkness!" Clifford began, rambling, splashing in. It was an old Marty Robbins song. "Ribbon of darkness… over me," and Clifford's voice, babbling, slogging, splashing. *If he can do it*, Woods thought, *so can I!*

Clifford's voice tumbled. It bobbed. Woods rose. He felt tethered. He stepped down off the bank and into the Salmon. The water felt colder, even against his waders. It felt rougher and less supportive than before. Clifford's burly voice ground out: "Fears I never had before—ribbon of darkness..." and Woods moved to close the gap.

He slid forward, the river's always-rearranging bedrock underfoot. Some rocks felt large and planted, some felt loose. And there was the river itself, uncoiling, first past Woods' upper calves, now his knees. Clifford sang: "Now she is gone from the meadow," unaware of Woods following him. He knew the words!

The river seemed so black! It seemed so provisional yet sweet! It seemed as if it could take Woods' life and forgive him at the same time! Woods started to giggle.

"Woods?" he heard Clifford's voice.

He couldn't stop giggling.

"Woods?"

Then Woods felt a surge, a lift—his upper thigh first, then his foot, and, as easy as breath, he was in the current, scudding off, heading down the river in the black—giggling, feeling the water on his face.

Clifford screamed his name: *Woods!* Then Woods swallowed water. Felt his head slam a rock.

When the light drifted in, Woods could see Clifford in it, strangely altered. Clifford was somewhere above, somewhere over, and the firelight, snapping, seemed to torture his face, to screw and buckle it into the face of a woman. "Hey, buddy," Clifford grinned. "Hey! Welcome! Welcome home!"

Could...yes!

Clifford *was* the woman: brows black, fully lined; lids that looked like hummingbirds; blush; foundation cream; blood-red lip gloss.

"How do you like me?" Clifford grinned.

Woods focused, or tried.

Clifford laughed. "The Aborigines!" he said, backlit.

What was he talking about?

"The Aborigines do this!" He seemed proud. "With their men," he said. "In the bush!" He preened. "At the point of Manhood!" He grinned. "They become women so they can become men! It's amazing!" Clifford laughed a lunatic laugh.

Woods' skull felt brutal. It felt slashed and emptied. His jaw ached.

"I cleaned you up," Clifford explained. "I thought of taking you in for stitches. But then I figured the hair would grow over where the rock got you, and—so to speak—it wouldn't matter."

Woods nodded. His face, the skin, felt stiff and coated.

Clifford explained the details: how he'd, in fact, tied the near end of the slashed river-rope to the back of Woods' wading suspenders just in case. *Just in case.* And how the rope had held and swung Woods, unconscious, back to the shore and made it quick for Clifford to find him. "Mouth to mouth!" Clifford explained. "Man to man! Mouth to mouth! CPR!" He kept grinning. Pleased.

Woods studied Clifford above in the firelight. He was gay and powerful; he was silly and strong. He looked like a clown and friend.

Clifford finished the rescue tale: tying off the new rope; carrying Woods back across, on his shoulders; dressing him in a set of dry clothes; treating his wounds. "And!" Clifford laughed.

"And?"

"And!" Clifford trumpeted, prolonging the drama.

"And what?" Woods said. "And what?" Then he realized: the stiffness in his face.

Clifford produced the mirror. Woods looked at himself. He was as Clifford was, and, as such, curiously attractive: not gaudy, not whorish. But tempting, comely. "I tried to be tasteful," Clifford said.

Woods said nothing. He looked at his eyes, especially. His lips. They were soft. He had never really seen them before. Woods had always thought his face to be something cut from grained wood or burlap, stuffed and padded. Blunt here, stubbled there; here an edge, there a surface. But none of that seemed true.

"How are you feeling?" Clifford asked.

"I'm...okay," Woods said.

Did Daria have lips like that? For Beth Ann?

Clifford told Woods that his pulse rate was perfect and his eyes clear. He said that the Aborigines spent the whole night in their "borrowed faces," and asked: would that be all right for the two of them? "Why stop here?" he said. "Why stop at the gate? When we can live in exile!" He laughed.

Woods thanked Clifford for saving his life.

"So?" Clifford said. "So? Till dawn?"

Woods agreed. He waited, at first, for Clifford to insert his own answer, but none came. Finally Clifford went on. "So, till dawn, then. We'll give ourselves till dawn. I mean, to find them. To find the women. Who are in us. Who are outside of us. I mean, true? To find a way in. Live beyond the pale! Dream beyond the gate!" Clifford laughed.

Inside the tent, they slipped into their sleeping bags. Woods' bones ached. He felt tears welling quickly. He could hear Clifford's relaxed breathing and the fine cracking of the fire snapping with its dry sparks outside. Woods' face streamed with wild, unknown gratitude and crazy bliss. He hugged himself inside his bag as he had seen Clifford do, earlier in the night, on the dance floor. He kissed the backs of his own hands. He kissed his wrists and fell asleep.

In the night, Woods dreamt that he and Beth Ann were in a bed. There were fish, swimming past them, resting on their bellies, flicking tails lazily with a mesmerizing, arrogant caution. And Woods felt some source of himself, some deeper well, fill, and though it was passion in part, it was something more than passion: it was beyond that, certainly beyond any question of making love. And Daria was there, sleeping, on the other side of the bed. Beyond their fish. Perhaps it was with some fish of her own. Or fish they shared. And Beth Ann seemed incredibly sweet, truly tender, talking about her life in ways she had stopped doing or, perhaps, had never done. And she stroked the fish.

Woods woke in the morning before Clifford. He ached and rose and walked himself to the river, where he lowered himself, through stiffness, to his haunches and looked down. The water circled yet held still; it gave back a face, a figure. And though the eddied face—unstable and half-lit in the small early drift—at once compelled and even amused Woods, he felt some ballast in his brain shift, the shift slapping a gyroscope at his uneasy center.

But then, before Woods could break the image, lift water, dissolve the woman, wash her back into the stream, he lost his vertical. And, in an almost slow-motion topple, found himself sitting—the Salmon moving around him—a mounded, mid-sized rock between his legs. It was a queer, puzzling moment—an act both inside and outside his brain—but Woods reached, seized the rock, strained it up, up, until it was there above him, over his head, shadowed and, backlit by the first sun, seeming to drip with blood. And it shocked Woods that a rock might appear so helpless and murderous in the same light.

They ate breakfast. It seemed huge and delicious. Clifford assembled eggs and sausages and pancakes. Coffee. He had removed his previous night's face as well. Then, again, all during the meal, their banquet, Clifford read a book Woods hadn't yet seen, the collected letters of the writer Flannery O'Connor. Clifford looked so... what was the word? So *pervaded*? Possibly, by the text as he read.

After breakfast, they broke camp, packed all their gear. Clifford helped Woods. He asked periodic questions about

Woods' skull, his neck: could he rotate it easily? His vision?

Then they were off—crossing the river for the final time, each using a walking stick, Woods' belt roped to the belt of Clifford *in the event...*

The cross was easy. The sun on the water, at nine in the morning, was unseasonably sweet and lustrous, warm and healing.

On the drive back to Sun Valley, climbing Galena Summit, they stopped at a small general store for coffee and for the view. The store had a rack of postcards. One of the cards showed what looked to Woods like a soft, mossy mouth in the mountainside, from which the clearest water rose in a kind of aerated brilliance. The card was labeled: *Headwater Of The River Of No Return.* Woods bought the card. He filled it out and posted it to Beth Ann at their home address. On it he wrote: "Where I've been."

THE LEGEND'S DAUGHTER

It seemed a starting place, so Tommy Bachman topped off his Cherokee and drove—into an eggplant-dim, wrinkled shadow of the mountains and toward Boise, chasing only a hunch, the faintest sense of Laura, his briefly known, sixteen-year-old stepdaughter, who, in one stroke, had earned her Idaho driver's permit, then stolen the test car.

Bachman's hunch involved a boatman named Rankin, a five-foot-ten, muscle knotyard of a young man, whom Laura'd met on a float from Stanley to Challis. Float season over, Rankin worked now as a bartender at a Boise wine bar, The Grape Escape. Laura loved teasing: "You watching? You watching, Tommy? Watch. Watch my Grape Escape! Rankin said I have a gift for pulling the cork." The night after Laura's and Rankin's float, they'd drunk beer, she'd told Bachman, in the hot tubs below Sunbeam.

"Were your clothes on?" Bachman had asked.

"Were our—excuse me, Tommy—*clothes on*? You mean, in the water?"

"You know what I mean," Bachman had said.

And Laura'd laughed, full cascade.

It had been a road with frost heaves—the tour of father and stepdaughter. It had been, pretty much, an unimproved highway. Bachman had tried, once, to be a musician in a band. Like ten thousand others, he'd had a steel guitar. But, like many, instead of being a musician, he'd become a drunk. Then a worse drunk. Then worse. Until, one day, he woke up in a smoking car—not really a car any more, just a frame around him, skeleton of a car, which had to have, somehow, burned around him while he sat blacked out, strapped into the driver's seat. *It's a miracle you're alive,* his friend Marshall had said. And it was. And so he stopped drinking, gave away his guitar, was given—for reasons lost somewhere in the night's drunken blackout—an immense insurance settlement.

After which, through a friend of a friend of Marshall's, he got a job caretaking the horse ranch of a movie producer whose name Bachman could never pronounce, just outside Hailey, off the road to Picabo. In his first caretaking month, he met Laura's mother, Stephanie, in the herbal tea section of Atkinson's in Ketchum. They'd talked for a good fifteen minutes about self-healing and alternative medicines. It was the first time Bachman had heard the word *chakra*. A month later, they married. The next month, Stephanie ran away with a steel guitar player from a band at Bruce Willis's Mint, leaving Laura behind.

Why? You're not my father! was a kind of song lyric Laura sang, daily almost, over the next year and a half. Help me dry the dishes? *Why? You're not my father.* And the second verse of the song was: *You can't make me!* You're not my father. You can't make me! Bachman had, in fact, suggested Laura put the words to music, she used them so much. *Hey, that's so funny I forgot to laugh,* Laura said.

So, here he was: in pursuit of a woman-child who abhorred him. Because, well, there wasn't really a reason—other than he wasn't a drunk any more. Other than Stephanie had been genuinely tender, for a month. And it had been the first tenderness Bachman had ever known. And so perhaps Bachman assumed Laura carried a tenderness too, somewhere within, and it shouldn't just be let loose on a highway somewhere, free to misunderstand itself and make a dozen wrong choices. Lowman spun by in the deep October dark, then New Centerville.

On the barely near side of midnight, Bachman discovered Boise's Grape Escape, parked, and ambled in. The mood inside was what Stephanie would have called *ambient*—not all that light, not entirely dark. No one looked like Laura. No one looked like Rankin. Bachman approached a bartender, wearing a nametag that read *Potter*.

"Rankin here still?" Bachman asked.

"Rankin took off," Potter—who, if Rankin had been tall, redheaded and forty, could have been Rankin—said.

"Gone, then? For the night?"

"No, gone…as in gone. He took off last week," the bartender, Potter, said.

"For?"

"No one knows. Jennifer, one of our servers, guesses Key West. 'Cause Rankin had Key West on his brain—talked about it. But he also had Anchorage. So, it's a split decision. Choose your hemisphere."

Bachman asked Potter if he, perchance, knew of a young woman named Laura, whether anyone named Laura had called recently, and Potter laughed.

"Right!" he said. "Which one?" He told Bachman Rankin would only see women named Laura. "My point is," Potter said, "if a woman calls for Rankin—it's Laura."

"This would be a sixteen-year-old Laura from Hailey," Bachman said, and he produced a picture.

"Fucking Rankin!" Potter said.

"Meaning?" Bachman said.

"Nothing. Just—asshole—he loves babies," Potter said. And he shook his head. Then laughed.

Bachman felt like hitting him, felt like climbing across the bar. But it wasn't Potter he wanted to hit. Potter, in his own way, was indignant, found Rankin shameful.

"Well, the point, I guess," Bachman said, "is this Laura's my step-daughter. She met Rankin on a river trip in August. Ran away. Today. Stole a state car. If she shows up—same way I showed up—looking for Rankin, here's a number. There's a machine. Leave a message, I'll be checking. And—I have no right to ask, you may not want to do this, but—try to keep her around, try to keep her in town. Stall her."

"Sure," Potter said. He took Bachman's slip. "Listen, can I get you a drink? Anything? We have a really nice '94 Mondavi Pinot Noir we're featuring. Husky. A little plumish. Has a lot of echo."

Bachman had no translation for Potter's words. He thanked him nevertheless, asked whether they had any Pacifica on tap—which they did—so Bachman ordered a schooner, sat at a table. The bar emptied. No one came in. "You're not drinking your beer," the server, Jennifer, said. "Something wrong with it?"

"It's beer," Bachman said.

"Sorry. I don't think I—"

"I just bought it to remember—not drink," Bachman said.

When he left, within a block, Bachman saw a small woman on the sidewalk, kicking, flinging something at a man hovering above her.

"Hey!" Bachman called out to the man and began closing the distance.

"Get this fucker away!" the woman yelled.

"Hey!" Bachman shouted again.

"Keep out, Jack!" the woman's assailant said. "Back off! This is a private matter."

"The fuck it is!" the woman shouted.

And now Bachman could see what the woman was hurling at the man—pieces of broken beer bottle lying by her side.

"Baby, I warned you!" The man lunged. He tried to shield himself, retreated.

Bachman had played high school football. Defense. He remembered squaring off on a target. And did that—twenty feet now, perhaps, away. He became a tackler. Another piece of glass flew.

"Bitch! Fucking bitch!" the man shouted.

Bachman exploded as Lou Rooney, his coach, had instructed: *Explode forward!* Bachman hit the man, drove him.

"Way to go!" he heard the woman say.

He felt a sharp, incisive pain, warm blood.

"Asshole!" the assailant said. And took off.

The woman's name was Lanie Lou Macklin. When Bachman took her hand and drew her up, she froze. "Jesus—your hands have got maps in them," she said. And then, favor for favor, she got Bachman to his Cherokee, drove them both to Holy Cross Emergency, where Bachman's shoulder stab got treated and stitched and Lanie Lou's attack reported.

"Where can I drive you? Where do you need to go?" Bachman asked, after, in the parking lot.

"You don't want to hear," Lanie Lou Macklin said. "*Where do I need to go?* That your question, Man With Maps In His Hands? Into the Wilderness!" she announced. "Into the Wilderness, Jocko!"

"Name's Bachman. Tommy Bachman."

"Into the Wilderness, Tommy Bachman, then. To find a man who will only be there and won't be anywhere else. Into the Wilderness to find my father."

"So?"

"Yes?"

"I don't know. I don't know, I guess, exactly, what wilderness you're talking about. The Frank D. Church Wilderness? Some other? Which wilderness?"

"Right! *Which wilderness*, indeed! Nice shot! Bullseye!" Lanie Lou Macklin laughed. It was the first time Bachman had heard anything in her voice that was like laughter. "Which—? Well let me tell you, he's gotten lost in them *all*! So the question is, which one *this* time—right? Which blackness to light a fire in? You tell me! Choose a wilderness and look! That's the thing I've been doing. Does a legend—hey! It's just a question! Does a legend, do you think, have a favorite wilderness?"

The Legend, it turned out, was Mackie Macklin, Lanie Lou's father—up there, out there, with Hank Williams, Jr. and Willie Nelson. Mackie Macklin had risen and risen—through the late 70s, the 80s, the early 90s. "Werewolf Heart." "Dry Dakota." "Frozen Margarita Memories." Bachman knew him, had tapes, CDs, played them daily sometimes. Somewhere around 1993, Mackie Macklin had stopped touring, stopped recording. "When a very visible person stops appearing in any way, you know—that oughta be a sign for most people, a signal," Lanie Lou said, "that that person will soon, in fact, disappear. Which is what my daddy, right after that, did. Poof! Gone! Anybody seen Mackie?"

Lanie Lou said that, at first, those close to Mackie thought alcohol—a kind of slough, depression. Then they thought possibly religion—that Mackie'd made a kind of peace with God, private, that he was keeping. "He got thinner for a couple of months. Then heavier," Lanie said. "He started parasailing—day, night, didn't matter, he paid people to fly him up. It didn't matter what time—you could look up, see Daddy in the sky. Until you couldn't. Until he was gone. The last time he played in public, he lit his Gibson on fire. Played it until it was ashes. Song called 'Shooting Star.'"

"Do you have leads?" Bachman asked.

"One! He would never leave the West," Lanie said. "So if that's a lead, a clue—I know that. I mean, I know there's no sense looking for him in, say, South Carolina."

"Beyond—"

"Beyond's a lead!" Lanie Lou interrupted. "Good! Jesus. Could I have found my mentor? Good for you! *Beyond*. I like that! He'll be some place *beyond*—for sure. Because he's—no question—a *beyond* kinda guy. He'll be in the West—and on the other side of something." She threw her head back. "FUCK!" she yelled at the Idaho stars. "MY DADDY'S BEYOND!" Then, to Bachman, "I'm sorry." Then, "So—two good leads—we're getting somewhere. It's amazing. Help me find him?"

Bachman explained his own quest.

"Well—then there's a pair of us, as somebody said. Know that poem?"

"I don't think so," Bachman said.

"Search and Rescue!" Lanie Lou said. "It's a poem called 'Search and Rescue' by Emily Dickinson—I'm just kidding. Search and rescue! Should we team up? It's conceivable, you know. They're together. The Legend's been known to—but that was in another country, possibly. And besides—you're not a reader, I can see," Lanie Lou said to Bachman.

"Not particularly," Bachman said. "Though I have nothing against it."

"I like you, Tommy," Lanie Lou said. "Something in the way you—"

"I'm not bad," Bachman said. "I'm not a bad person."

"I know. I can tell that," Lanie Lou said.

Lanie Lou pointed them to a 24-hour After the Bars Close Café. They sat in a booth, drank coffee. Bachman ordered a waffle. Lanie Lou grew silent, kept dipping the tips of her fingers into her black coffee. Bachman watched her.

"You cold?" he asked finally.

"Not that I know of, no one's ever complained," Lanie Lou said, staring out the window, then at Bachman. "You're not a raving comedian, I can see," she said.

"I suspect not—or suspect so," Bachman said. "Besides, someone told me once that comedy was timing."

"It seems reasonable."

"And I think, probably, I lack—"

"Right," Lanie Lou said.

"Timing," Bachman finished.

"The old Timing," Lanie Lou said. "The old Timing." And she smiled.

They bought an *Idaho Statesman.* On the front page of the second section was an article about a sixteen-year-old woman who had washed up ten miles down from Twin Falls on the banks of the Snake. She'd been assaulted and tossed, police guessed, over the rim of the Grand Canyon. She was carrying a recent driver's permit, but her name was being withheld until notification of next-of-kin. Lanie Lou spotted the article, took a breath, slid it to Bachman. "I don't mean to be the Angel of...you-tell-me, but I think you ought to read this," she said.

Bachman did, stuffed his fist into his mouth—bit it, biting it harder and harder.

"Must be your own teeth still—you've drawn blood," Lanie Lou said. "Not the smartest move in the world, I should add, given those teeth've been active in an After the Bars Close waffle." She reached into her purse for an alcohol wipe and for Kleenex. "Whatever the stars—you're clearly into blood-letting, though, tonight."

Bachman stood.

"Tommy! Hey, Tommy—"

"I need—I have to make a call," Bachman said. And he moved unsteadily to the entry, where there was a payphone.

Lanie Lou followed. "Tommy—at least, you know, use the wipe, stuff the Kleenex against where you bit. You're going to—"

Bachman did as requested, said nothing, made his call, listened. Finally, he hung up. "I have three phone messages," he said. "From the state barracks in Twin Falls." Lanie Lou had her hands, palms flat, against his back.

"Tommy—I'm sorry," she said.

They stood that way, silent, for ten minutes.

Maybe Bachman would understand, maybe he wouldn't, Lanie Lou said, but she really needed to be with him when he drove over to Twin Falls for the identification. Which she did. Which he did. A pulp, really—Laura—a jelly, a mass, a slug, a once-beautiful woman-child made ugly. And two days later, when Bachman spoke at a special memorial service at Wood River Regional High, Lanie Lou was with him still, listening shyly to him telling the juniors and seniors about his own flight, own fire, own crash; how you can want a life and to escape a life at the same time, get confused. "It's hard to find people," he ended. "It's just—" and he started to cry, not knowing why. "Hard, very hard to find people."

On their way to his Cherokee in the Wood River parking lot, Lanie Lou held Bachman's arm like the spar of a ship. And she didn't say anything. And she didn't say anything. Until, finally, "So—Tommy, now. What now?" she said. "What do you say? Us two? The two of us? Try to find the Legend? Go Beyond?"

In the car, Bachman rolled his window down. The air was oaky and chilled and damp, like chardonnay.

"If you lose someone, you should find someone—don't you think?" Lanie Lou asked. "Doesn't that seem—I don't know—kind of irrefutable? Lose someone—find someone? Go for symmetry? Would the Universe play dice with God? Sorry, did I just turn something around? Hey, every kid in that auditorium heard you today, you know. Heard you. Including myself. Every one."

"Come home," Bachman said. "With me tonight. I've got fresh corn. I don't drink anymore, but whatever you drink—I'll get. And I'll grill us—you eat meat?"

Lanie Lou smiled. "Whatever," she said. "Sure. Long's it's not red; sure, sure, I'll go home with you."

"Then tomorrow I'll help."

"Baby—" Lanie Lou shook her head. "Baby—you're help now. You're help now, you just don't know it.

Lanie Lou drank Stags' Leap cabernet from a jelly glass,

sat behind Bachman—legs astride—while he shucked corn. "What a sweet night," she said. "What a sweet man you are. And I have to say—your body's like...like it's got the program for a smart missile or something. It's bizarre—the ways it points me."

"If I kiss you later—will you mind?" Bachman asked.

"Oh! No, I won't mind," Lanie Lou said. "I won't—no, you won't get any objection from me." And she leaned her head into the curl of Bachman's shoulders and tried not to cry.

Bachman built a fire in his stone fireplace. They ate. Lanie Lou undid his shirt. They kissed, made love, lay on the rug, heads on pillows. "It's been a while for me," Bachman said.

Lanie Lou took his hand and kissed it.

"No comment?" Bachman asked.

Lanie Lou shook her head. "It's hard enough to find people. A man said that once," she said.

"Was I all right?" Bachman asked.

"Stop it," Lanie Lou said. "Stop it, just stop it. Right now. Stop it."

They slept skin-to-skin in Bachman's wide bed—the room roiled with woodsmoke and with the raw stone smell of its walls. "You're so young!" Bachman said at one point.

"Possibly—but don't bet the ranch on it, Tommy," Lanie Lou said.

In the morning, they made love again, slept, made love before Bachman slipped out, brewed coffee, steeped Irish oatmeal.

"You know—your skin's a gyroscope," Lanie Lou called. She was washing her hair in the bathroom sink.

"Explain that to me later," Bachman said.

"I think I'm keeping you," Lanie Lou said.

"Let's go find the Legend," Bachman said.

"I don't know," Lanie Lou said.

"What do you mean?" Bachman asked.

"I mean I don't know. The point's possibly moot."

"I'm not sure I—"

"It's okay; talk happens. I'm talking to myself." And she joined him at his stove. "Something about your skin," Lanie Lou said.

Inside the Cherokee, Lanie Lou slipped her hand under Bachman's fresh blue denim shirt. "I'll say, it scares me—believing what I'm believing. But just drive. Drive; go; start out."

Bachman did.

"Turn left. Right now. Don't ask questions. Take Idaho 75 south." When they got to the junction of Idaho 75 and U.S. 84, Lanie Lou said, "Good, now 84 west."

"I'm not sure I get exactly what you're doing," Bachman finally said.

"I'm not sure exactly what I'm doing either. Except your skin's a map; your skin's got this freaky GPS or something. Installed, somehow, into it. And I'm just paying attention. I'm just getting the word."

"My skin's—?"

"Shut up, Tommy. I'm sorry. I don't mean *shut up*. I just mean...shut up. I learn by going where I have to go—okay? You know, it pisses me off—losing all these allusions."

"I'll say—I have to say, I don't know what you're talking about," Bachman said.

"Right. Yes. Exactly," Lanie Lou said. "Exactly! Okay, okay. North in three miles. Idaho 55."

Bachman did as instructed. They took Idaho 55, bypassing Boise, driving through Horse Shoe Bend, Placerville, Banks and Smith's Ferry. To the east, to the west, farmers burned their fields, making the sky, the light, a gauzy green. "You know, I have to tell you, I'm scared," Lanie Lou said. "I'm scared as shit about all of this."

"Except—I don't know what *all of this* is," Bachman said.

“Your skin. The map. The messages,” Lanie Lou said.

“My skin? The map? The messages?” Bachman repeated.

“Your skin. The map. The messages,” Lanie Lou said.

They drove twenty minutes in silence. It was four in the afternoon, light the color of alfalfa dust, magpies wherever there was roadkill.

“Anyone ever use you as a Rand McNally before?” Lanie Lou asked.

“I don’t even know what you’re talking about,” Bachman said.

“I think where we’re going—where Beyond is—is McCall,” Lanie Lou said.

“Fourteen miles,” Bachman said.

“That’s what your back says.”

“That’s what my *back* says?”

“McCall,” Lanie Lou said.

When they entered McCall, Lanie Lou’s hand on Bachman’s back started to shake. “What’s the matter?” Bachman asked.

“It’s terrible, you know? You want something, then, when you get close, what you’ve wanted scares the shit out of you. You think, *I don’t want this after all.* It’s too big. It’s too true.”

“You know, yesterday—”

“I don’t think I want you to talk.”

“Yesterday—I don’t think I had any trouble understanding you. Today—”

“I grow—I grow on people, Tommy. Sometimes close. Sometimes away. Nevertheless—”

“I felt close this morning,” Bachman said.

“Always trust the morning,” Lanie Lou said. “Always trust—left here! *Left*. We’re going to circle the lake. We’re going to dance the orange in a manner of speaking—oops! There I go again.”

Bachman signaled left, turned. McCall Lake was the bluest turquoise—cumulus floating, veins of gold running through.

Ducks sailed. There were bands of Canada geese.

"Pull over!" Lanie Lou said.

Bachman complied. And they sat on the shoulder for a half hour, Lanie Lou's head bowed, eyes shut, Bachman wondering if she were awake, even. He felt reluctant to speak, to jar anything; the envelope holding them seemed that fragile, tremulous.

Shadows came. Dark. Thickness to the silence. "Tommy, turn the radio on," Lanie Lou said, finally.

Bachman did. Mackie Macklin's "Werewolf Heart" played. "Jesus H. Fucking Christ," Lanie Lou said, and began hyperventilating.

"Anything—"

"Tommy, shut up—okay?" Lanie Lou said.

"I can do?" Bachman finished.

"Breathe with me. Let me breathe; breathe with me," Lanie Lou said.

"Maybe you don't—" Bachman began.

"Maybe I don't. That's right," Lanie Lou said. "And that's what I'm thinking: maybe I only thought I did—but I don't. So let the wine-that's-me breathe—okay? It was a good year and a bad year: let the wine breathe."

Bachman did.

"There'll be a roadhouse," Lanie Lou began. And she described a tavern with a dirt lot. "Lots of Oly signs. Front porch with a railing busted through at least a hundred times. Shit carved into the door. Pickups. Harleys. Dogs in the beds of pickups. Sidecars on half the Harleys. Cars all put together from other cars. The smell of fry grease. Ashes always—that smell: something beyond fire, burned out. Weeds. And he won't be there," Lanie Lou said. "My daddy, the Legend. Won't be there. But he will just have *been* there. I'll begin to describe, and people will say, That was Mackie Macklin? He was just here! And they'll begin a story—wild-ass story, wilderness story. And it'll break even your heart—listening."

"What do you mean, break even *my*—?"

"They're just words. Okay? Leave me alone. I'm just talking; they're just words. Just—! Don't question me. Don't question everything. Hey, I'm sorry. I'm tight. I'm tense. Fifteen years! A lot of water...wherever, under—whatever. I can never remember the clichés—doesn't that just frost your ass? Just the lines of the songs, the poems—which no one recognizes. Or most don't. Hey, you know who wrote the Legend's lyrics, Tommy? Mackie Macklin's? At the age of thirteen, fourteen? Are you following me? Do I have to tell you? No, I don't have to tell you. I can read your eyes. Right, me. So, can you guess what it feels like? Driving through the night at the age of—we're less far apart than you think—whatever, and hearing your own words from your disappeared daddy's lips over an all-night radio? Is that a rhetorical question? I don't know. How'd we get here anyway? Oh, that's right, your back."

Again, the gelatin, the voiceless dark, set in.

"So, well then. Shall we?" Lanie Lou finally said.

"You tell me. I'm just here, I'm just the driver," Bachman said.

"Yes, you are, you certainly are," Lanie Lou said. "And so the answer is yes. Turn the key, fire the ignition, head on down, etcetera. Thank you. Please."

Within three miles, Lanie Lou asked Bachman to roll down his window. He did. The air was filled with ash, with smoke.

"Oh Christ! Oh, fuck. Oh Christ!" Lanie Lou said.

"What're you thinking?"

"What'm I knowing's more the point," she said. "Oh, kiss my ruby-red—! Shit!"

"I don't—"

"All will be revealed!" Lanie Lou said. "All will be revealed," she pointed ahead, "around that bend!"

And then, as called, around the bend, hard right, sat a charred structure in a sprawled gravel lot—bones only, framing, anatomy.

"Roadhouse!" Lanie announced. "Ah-ha! The fabled roadhouse of my monologue! Jesus, Tommy, don't drive past, asshole! Pull in, *pull in!*"

Which Bachman did—Lanie Lou leaping out into the Cherokee's lights, sweeping left, right, calling out, "Mackie Macklin was here! Mackie Macklin was here!" up and wide and out and into the sky.

Bachman could read the sign, separate, framed beyond all the smoldering wreckage: Grizzly's Watering Hole.

He killed the car, turned the headlights off, couldn't move at first, just sat, watched Lanie Lou, the Legend's daughter, throwing stones now—little ones at first, then huge ones, boulders—into the incinerated tavern. *So what did she think she was doing?* Bachman wondered. *What were the stones about?*

He got out, walked near, stood. Lanie Lou was bent over, hands on her knees. She was coughing, lungs clotted, frayed.

"Can I—?" Bachman began.

But Lanie Lou, back to him, raised her hands, waved them.

Bachman stopped. Waited. Lanie stood, feet spread. He could see her shoulders broaden, then taper, until her breath quieted, became regular.

"I can imagine the story," she said, not turning. "And I can imagine a good one, a whopper—but it won't even be close. It'll be in the galaxy. I always manage the right galaxy—just don't ever get near." She turned and faced Bachman, smiled at him. "Not the day you'd planned—right?" she said.

"That's more than often the case," Bachman said. "Not the life I'd planned, but—what the hell."

"I like you, Tommy," Lanie Lou said. "I could write you songs—if you sang, if you played, if you had the slightest clue about music." She coughed; she laughed. "You could be a Legend." Then she started to cry.

She came to Bachman, let him hold her, sobbed, growled like an animal, hit his back with her fists. "Goddamn your skin," she said. "Its heat, its compass, goddamn it. Goddamn it for bringing me here." And she moaned and growled into Bachman's shoulder, bit his neck. "You haven't bled in a while," she said. Laughed. Laughed with her crying, one with the other, hard to know which was which.

And then Bachman saw something, a shift in the dark over Lanie Lou's shoulder: over and past the sad matchsticks of the tavern and out on the lake. At first it looked like a light—a house, perhaps—across some bay: all the lights on, picture window. But the light jumped too much, rolled down itself into itself, then leapt. And Bachman realized that what he was seeing was some sort of craft, some sort of boat, powerboat, he imagined, on fire. And what he thought to say was: *Look*! But he hesitated. Lanie Lou'd had enough flames today, he thought, but then he wondered—though he had no real clue to what his wondering meant, *could that be? Enough flames?* So, "Look," he said. "Lanie. Look." And he pointed.

Lanie Lou loosed herself and turned, looked out. She drew a breath. "It never stops," she said.

They heard guitar music. Coming from—? The mind closes whatever gaps, tries its best to make a connection. But the guitar music simply wouldn't be in the burning boat. It was too near, too close. A voice spoke.

"Needed, I guess, another person," the voice said. It was at the edge of the lot—in shadows, shrubbery, trees. And, at the same instant, Bachman and Lanie Lou turned, observed. "Couldn't do it alone," the voice said.

"Da—!" Lanie Lou began. Her voice froze.

Bachman made out a shape, a figure. Standing at the edge of the lot where the aspen and lodgepole tangled together. It was a large figure—its shape suggesting it wore a coat or jacket, Stetson hat.

"I wondered whether we'd ever—" the voice went on, deep and grainy. "I've closed the space myself—far more times than you'll ever imagine. Seen you in a dozen Albertsons lots. Watched your shape at a window. Driven behind you in traffic. In front—checked you in my rear-view. But it always seemed—anyway—hooked up with another person, and here we are. So—what I want to say, and—don't try to get any closer, closer than you are, because I won't say it then. But what I want to say is, thank you for your songs—okay? Thank you for your words. You have a gift—and I was nothing, really, until I had them, your words. Because then I had *my* words too, your words gave me *my* words. So, Lanie, Lanie Lou, what's your friend's name? What's your name, friend?"

"Bachman," Bachman said.

"Tommy," Lanie Lou said.

The shape shifted. The mulching of small, dry branches snapping.

"Don't—" Lanie Lou began.

"Should I play something for you?" the voice said. "New?"

"Sure," Lanie Lou said. "Fine."

"Friend? Tommy?"

"Sure. Fine," Bachman said.

"Got a match?" the shape said.

"Not funny, Daddy," Lanie Lou said.

"Okay. Okay," the shape said. "New song. No flames. No hands. Came to me couple of days ago—on the wind. Hurtling—but I caught it. It's called—long, for a title, but it works—called 'See? You're Not My Father.'"

And, in the liquid night, spinning light, the shape played—voice a wanderer, out from the shadows to the blackened rafters of the shabby tavern, notes like lust, words like light, voice like ashes—while his daughter's hand, under Bachman's blue denim shirt, rode the gyroscope of her friend's skin.

THE MAN WHO MIGHT HAVE BEEN MY FATHER

When I was in the fifth grade at Walt Whitman Elementary in Brooklyn, my mother, who worked at a place called Rodeo, nights, and tried out for plays during the day, pulled me out of school and said we were going on a trip. It was October, just after the Olympics, and it seemed all my mother could talk about was Florence Joyner. She said boys should be excited about Florence Joyner too. Okay—if you say so.

My mother had been writing to a man in Idaho. A lot of days, I'd get the mail before she would, and there'd be one of his letters. They came in fat little white envelopes, which, most of the time, looked dirty. In one corner, they'd say: B. Mitchell, with a box number and then: Sunbeam Springs, Idaho. When I asked, she always said, "He's a man," (which I'd figured), or, sometimes, "Honey, we just write."

I asked if they'd ever met. She said, "Not really." She said it was crazy: one time, she'd been making a phone call to New Jersey and wasn't watching and dialed the wrong code and got this B. Mitchell, "Buddy," (right!) way off in Idaho. And they had talked. And she, I guess, had said enough so that, the next week, *he'd* called *her*. And that had started it, their speaking and writing back and forth for almost three years. And so it was B. Mitchell who she had taken me out of Walt Whitman for (which didn't thrill me). She had gotten a cheap car too, and we were going to be driving out to some place called Sunbeam Springs in Idaho to see him.

I had never had a father. Which was fine. My mother said

he'd been "an indiscretion." She said, "Theater people sometimes *do* things." Right. My mother was good, though. She was unusual. And pretty. And she could always surprise a person, which I liked, with a different voice or song or something. We would walk everywhere, and I would look and she would be, usually, the most interesting person wherever we went.

She said her monologues to me. The ones she did when she auditioned. She said them to me all over. Sometimes at home, going to bed; sometimes in the park by the bridge; sometimes, if it wasn't too crowded, in the subway. She did *Antigone*, and she did Beatrice from Shakespeare. She did Nina from *The Seagull*; she did someone called the Princess from a play called *Extremities.* Her voice would go all over, everywhere, up and down. She'd laugh; I'd laugh. She'd cry and she'd get me sometimes (though I never told her).

"How long does it take to get to Idaho?" I asked. I was thinking about all the soccer games in the park I'd be missing.

"I'm not sure," she said.

"Did B. Mitchell *ask* you?" I said.

"More or less," she said. "B. Mitchell opened it up."

I nodded.

"I have to say," and she did a funny thing, lifting her eyes. "He certainly opened the possibility up. And I earned a little money this summer. From that commercial. So why not spend it, right?"

"I guess so," I said.

"And I'm not getting any younger, either—am I?" she said. Then she said, like it was only half a question, "So..."

I had never really been with her in a car. It was a Honda. Where the paint was still on, it was blue. It was actually *two* colors: some places blue, some places brownish. And it had silver tape on one of the back windows where jerks, I'm sure, had tried to break in. She'd parked it a block from our apartment on Bergen Street, and I got to pack some clothes and books and a sketch pad in a Safeway bag. She put some clothes into a suitcase for herself and some cold pizza and some fruit and some sandwiches in another bag, and we headed off.

It was night. The car smelled like a stuffed chair and made, I suppose, the usual car noises but also a noise sort of like grating carrots. "This may be touch and go," my mother said as we crossed the bridge. I thought: *we're not even going to get to Pennsylvania.*

There was no radio in the car; it had been ripped out, and there was just a hole, but we'd brought the Quasar, and it played our tapes. My mother had a hundred plays on tape, but she didn't play those the first night. She played Anne Murray and Reba McEntire. And then Willie Nelson. "It's where we're going, honey," she said. "It's where we're going. I like the music."

I fell asleep. But before I fell asleep I remember the lights of New York, across the bridge, getting yellower and yellower and more and more like I was seeing them through a spider web. Meanwhile Reba McEntire was singing "The Sweetest Gift." I remember my mother, with her arm around me, her hand patting my head. How she started singing: *It was a halo sent down from Heaven.* I remember she stopped her singing and said—except it was to herself and I could tell that she probably thought I was asleep already—"Oh, Sweet Jesus. What am I getting into?"

When I woke up, it was still dark, and my mother was still driving. Now humming. My head was on her lap, the rest of my body out along the seat. "What time is it?" I asked. Her face was looking small, floating and white. She gave me a pat but kept looking ahead. "It's late," she said. "It's definitely late." She laughed.

"Are we stopping?" I asked.

"I don't know," she said.

I didn't understand.

"I suppose sometime," she said. "I suppose sometime we'll stop." She laughed again. "I mean, I guess we'll have to."

"Where are we?" I asked.

"Ohio!" she said, as if it were in one of her monologues. "Ohio!" as if the word were funny.

"How old is B. Mitchell?" I asked.

"His name is Buddy," she said.

"I know," I said.

"Buddy Mitchell!" She said his name the way she'd said Ohio. It was the way *I* would have said it. "Buddy Mitchell, of Sunbeam Springs, Idaho!" And she pulled a face.

"So, okay, how *old* is he?"

"Oh...thirtyish," she said and then smiled. "Or thirty-something."

"Thirty-one?" I asked.

"Thirty-two, thirty-three, thirty-eight, nine…forty. Somewhere there." She was twenty-nine; I was twelve. "I asked him once," she said. "'Are you on the downside of forty-five?' And he said, 'Yes.' Would you like to stop?" she asked me.

"I guess," I said. "Where would we do that?"

"I'll find a motel," she said.

The motel was called the Piker Motel, and it had a red and green sign that would have seemed small in Brooklyn but seemed huge, actually, where it was—I guess still in Ohio—because there were no other lights, only trees and the motel itself anywhere near. It was okay. The room and television were bigger than our apartment and television on Bergen Street—except it was three in the morning and there weren't, really, any programs on.

"Good night, honey," my mother said. She reached across from her bed to mine.

"Are you going to marry B. Mitchell?" I asked.

She didn't say anything.

"Mom?" I said.

"Idaho's a long way," she said.

"So, then would I have a father?" I asked. It seemed weird, the whole idea: some guy, sitting in our kitchenette, asking me to eat more of my artichoke or something.

My mother did something then, when I asked that question about would-I-have-a-father. She did something with her breath, sucked it a funny way. Then breathed out. Then sucked in again. I waited. "Stranger things have happened," she said. And then fell off to sleep. I think, actually, she may have said it a second time. It was habit of hers, saying things twice. "Stranger things have happened."

I went back to sleep. But before I did, I found my sketchpad and tried to do a drawing of B. Mitchell—what I thought he might look like. I gave him kind of a beard. And sideburns.

I got put in charge of the map. It was okay. I had this friend in Brooklyn, Pinky, who collected atlases, and he would have *loved* it, but it was probably better than my doodling all the time and imagining more B. Mitchell faces on my sketchpad.

We were on I-80, except it was also I-90. It was early in the morning, and we were going past towns in the state of Indiana with names like Nevada Mills and Hudson Lake. And then it was noon, and it was like New Jersey, except not because it was still Indiana, a place called Gary. And then it was Chicago—on a lake and in Illinois. And then, in the afternoon, after we stopped at a place called Taco Burger and had something which made my mother laugh, called *huevos McMuffin*, it was just I-90 and the towns we rode past and past some more were called things like Elgin and Winnebago and Woodbine.

The Judds were playing; my mother really liked "The Sweetest Gift." But there was also George Strait and Marty Robbins and Emmylou Harris. And then we changed again—states—this time into Wisconsin, hundreds of towns, all with Indian names—Tomah and Onalaska and Winona—and my mother started doing monologues. Reba McEntire was doing "My Mind Is On You," and the town of White Creek was just out the window and it was getting dark, and my mother suddenly rolled down her window and yelled out, "I am what became of your child!" and then told me it was from a play called *Night,*

Mother. It was pretty amazing.

The car wasn't sounding very good. It was making little spits and big rattles. At first my mother said, "Don't listen. Just read the map." But then the car noises began coming more and sounding louder. So by St. Charles, in Minnesota, my mother pulled into a Chevron, where a man with *Carl* on his suit said he'd "give it a shot." It was seven at night, so we got a room at the Whitewater Motel, which had a big, yellow rubber raft on the roof, over our room.

It was nice; it was okay. My mother called and told the man, Carl, at the Chevron, where we were, and we went out for pizza, which was okay, except not as good as the pizza at Ray's on Sixth Avenue. It was all right though, for Minnesota pizza. We brought it back to our room and watched *Moonlighting*. I added a scar to one of B. Mitchell's faces, then erased it.

My mother seemed nervous. She kept looking at the phone and getting up and going into the bathroom and running the water and coming back and standing and watching the screen and going to the motel window and pulling the curtains back and looking out.

"Does B. Mitchell..." I started to say something, but stopped. My mother looked at me. I started in again. "Does B. Mitchell know we're coming?" I asked.

"He does," she said. Then repeated it. Then looked back, out, toward the street.

"Have you called him?" I said.

"Have I called him when?" she said, and I could see her biting her lip.

"Have you called him on our trip?"

"Not yet," she said.

"Should you?" I asked.

She looked like she was mad then, like she couldn't figure my question. "Sometime," she said finally. "Of course. Sometime. Eventually."

"Do you think Carl will be able to fix our car?" I said.

"Honey..." Sometimes she would tell me not to push something. That was a favorite expression. *Honey, don't push it.* "Not so many questions, okay? Please, tonight," she said. So I said *sure* and went back to *Hawk* on television.

I don't think my mother slept very well. I almost think I heard her crying. I lay in bed with light the color of some Chinese restaurant fish tank water sneaking through the curtains, and I kept trying to picture B. Mitchell, except he came and went. He was sort of short at first. Then tall. Then he had a checked shirt on. Red and black. No tie. He looked pretty serious. Except, sometimes, he would smile. He also had on a pair of boots. With long laces. And his hair wasn't all that combed. And then he had a beard, but the beard went away except just a little, like the first time I'd drawn him, because he probably needed to shave. And then he had one of those vests on. Like the sleeping bags. When we'd gone out on the streets, in St. Charles, for pizza, there'd been a lot of guys with those vests. *Down,* my mother told me. And then his face was lumpy, but okay. What I mean is: with edges, like a rock. It was all right. And his eyes were dark. And he had, like, really big, bushy eyebrows. I did a page, just of eyebrows, in my sketchpad. Then I fell asleep.

The next day Carl told us the "bad news." It was going to cost a lot to fix up what was wrong. "If you can give me another day, though, with the rascal, then I think I can do 'er," he said. Then smiled. He had what my mother guessed was zucchini on his teeth. "I've done a kind of baling wire job in the meantime," he said. "Just in case."

"That will have to do," my mother said.

"It might hold," he said. "It might not."

My mother thanked Carl and paid him, and when we started the car up, it sounded better.

It wasn't a good day, though. We were still in Minnesota, and it was raining. It was *really* raining, and the windshield wipers didn't work all that well. My mother had to lean forward and put her face almost against the windshield to drive. She started crying around Dexter. "Honey—don't mind me," she said. "I just need to cry a little. It's like the rain—I just need to *do* this for a while and get it out of my system."

I felt bad.

We had to drive pretty slowly. Near another town called Blue Earth, the car started to go *thump-thump-thump-thump.*

We had a flat tire. She pulled over. She just sat for a while, with the engine running, moving her tongue around on the inside of her teeth, doing back-and-forth things with her jaw. "Okay," she said finally. "Okay, I can do this. It's a flat tire. Why is it seeming like a problem? I just jack the car. I wrench the lugs. I lift one tire off, put the other one on, tighten the nuts again, we're on our way. This is not a problem. Are you feeling strong?" she asked me. I said yes.

"Are you feeling like my right-hand man?" she asked.

I said yes again. What was she asking?

It was really raining.

We got out. She opened the trunk. She bent forward and just stared in. She stood up straight. She wrapped her arms around herself like a person who's cold, which she may have been. "I don't believe this," she said. "This isn't true. People don't sell other people cars without jacks and tools." She took deep breaths. Her blond hair dripped down over her face like weeds. She stared some more into the open trunk and then shut it and said, "I'm sorry. Back into the car."

I followed her.

She put our dim lights on. We sat a long time before a man driving a pipe truck stopped and asked what the matter was. She told him. Then the truck driver looked at me. "How far are you going?" he asked. My mother said Idaho. The truck driver looked at me a couple more times. He was a skinny guy in a blue moving suit. "Let me see if I can rouse anybody in Fairmont," he said. And then, to my mother, "You want to sit with me in my cab while I make the call?"

"Isn't that a winch on the front of your cab?" my mother said.

"You know what a winch is?" he asked.

"Isn't that one?"

"Well—I believe it is!" he said. He looked angry. He looked at me again. He looked frustrated.

"And it looks like you've got a cable on it," my mother said.

"Well, so it does!" he said and looked even angrier.

"Do you have tools?"

"I might," he said.

My mother wouldn't let him help. She just asked him to lift our car with his winch and cable and then let us use his tools. She and I changed our tire in his headlights there in the rain, while he sat in his cab, not looking happy. I loved it, sort of. I loved *something* about it. I'm not sure. It was sometime in the afternoon. The rain in all the trees sounded like paper bags rattling. I pushed the wrench with her and helped her lift the one tire off and next tire on. My mother's hands got so red that I asked her if they were bleeding but she said no.

And then she leaned in, with the rain over both our faces, and gave me a kiss. When we finished the tire and looked up, there was a deer who'd come out of the woods and to the edge of the road on the other side. With antlers! And he didn't look wet at all. He knew we were there. "Oh!" my mother said. "Oh, my God isn't he beautiful!"

My mother gave the skinny truck driver twenty dollars when he lowered and disconnected us from the cable.

"Who do you think I am?" he said.

"I have no idea," my mother said.

"I didn't stop for the money," he told her. My mother looked like she was going to say something, then didn't. He kept pinching his nose with his thumb and his next finger.

"Do you have any children?" my mother asked him.

Now *he* looked like he would almost say something. "My ex-wife has a boy and a girl," he said.

"Keep the twenty," my mother said. "A wrecker would have cost more."

The trucker eyed the twenty. I wanted him to look like a nicer person. Maybe that night I'd draw him and make him a nicer person. Except his hands were the color of motor oil. "You know the problem with today's women?" he asked.

My mother said she had no idea.

"They *do* everything," the trucker said.

"We're just trying to share the blanket," my mother said.

"With what?" the trucker said.

"Well, right now, I'm not sure," my mother said.

"My point exactly," the trucker said, and he held up an index finger with a black nail.

"Maybe it would be better if we all got out of this rain," my mother said.

And we did.

My mother played a Whitney Houston tape for about the next hundred miles, through towns like Imogene and Sherburn and Spafford. I thought that probably that night, wherever we were, in whatever motel, I'd get my pad and sketch the trucker, and probably get all the little twists in his face pretty right. Or maybe I'd put the trucker's—maybe just the nose—on B. Mitchell.

It started raining less. Then less. Which was good, because it was dark now, and before we knew it, it wasn't raining at all, and there were stars, even—way up through the windshield and an almost-full moon. My mother rolled down her window. It was cold. And I said that: I said, "Mom, it's pretty cold," and she said, "Honey, I know but just let me drive a while letting it in." So that was fine.

She changed our Whitney Houston for our Marty Robbins and began to smile. "You must be hungry," she said.

I said I was.

"Next place," she said.

The next place was Magnolia, with a café called the Split

Rock Ranch.

"I'm ordering a steak," my mother said. "We're in the West, so I'm ordering a steak. Maybe you'd like one."

"But you never eat meat," I said.

"We're twenty miles from South Dakota," my mother said.

I didn't get it.

"Once I ate meat," she said. "I may do it again—I may do it again!" she laughed.

The steaks were good. Our waitress's name was Cornelia. She had red hair and cheeks like pancakes. We had pie and ice cream afterwards.

"I feel really good tonight," my mother said. "I feel really positive and glad we did this."

"It's fun," I said. I said it to make her feel good. Still, it wasn't that much of a lie. "Have you called B. Mitchell?" I asked.

"Tonight, we sleep in South Dakota," she said. "Isn't that a great name for a state—South Dakota?" We stayed in Brandon. "Big day tomorrow!" my mother said.

And it was. We went totally across South Dakota and into Livingston, Montana. In South Dakota, we kept going past national grasslands: Fort Pierre National Grasslands, Buffalo Gap National Grasslands. All they *were* were *grass*. Better than the Badlands, which had been all sand, all *rock*. Still, even in the rain, I think I liked Minnesota better. In Minnesota you could see places where people lived, houses with porches.

But my mother was happy. She was singing with The Judds. She was singing with Emmylou Harris and with Willie Nelson and with George Strait and calling all these different monologues out the window. "They're from *Fool For Love*," she said. I remember one line—she kept saying it: "She was trespassing! She was crossing this forbidden zone but couldn't help herself!" She almost *sang* the line. She was really happy.

We spent that night in Livingston, Montana. "This is where we drop down," my mother said. "Tomorrow we drop down through Yellowstone and into Idaho, and I want to see it."

"Will we see the fire?" I asked. I think we'd talked about the fire in school.

"We probably will," she said.

"It won't still be burning though, right?" I said.

"No, I think it's all out," she said. "I think it's all out there now. I think they put it out so they could focus on the Olympics." And she laughed.

Our motel was called The Red Dog, but he wasn't around—there was just an orange cat when we checked in. It was sort of like a barn, The Red Dog; it had boards on the wall. And camera pictures of different men catching trout. They were interesting pictures. The men looked really glad they'd caught the fish they were holding. I wondered if any of them had kids along on their trips. With them. Catching the fish. I wondered if any of the kids had taken any of the pictures.

I drew my own hand in my sketchbook. Then I drew a fish in it. I thought: *this is me with a trout.* I imagined B. Mitchell beside me in a picture, standing there with his hand on my shoulder.

"Do you know what we'd have done if I were rich and famous and a lady of leisure?" my mother asked.

I said didn't know.

"If I were rich and famous and a lady of leisure," she said, "we'd be staying tonight at a place with a heated indoor pool. And at this very moment I'd be doing the backstroke."

"What would I be doing?" I said.

"That's a good question," she said. "Maybe drawing me doing the backstroke. Maybe jumping off the high board."

We had Italian food at a place called Gambini's. My mother said it was a joke, the restaurant name, but the food tasted good. She had something called angel hair pasta that she said was perfect. And garlic bread. She kept asking for more garlic bread. "What have I got to lose, right?" she said to the waiter.

He said, "It cures everything."

"Then I'm in great shape," my mother said, and stuffed another piece into her mouth.

We had wine, too. They brought it in what they called a *carafe*, and I had a whole glass. When my mother finished the carafe, someone brought another. Also, one of the things about Gambini's was the pool table, where, sometimes, people played, sometimes they didn't. So when they weren't, and there was no more garlic bread and just a half-a-carafe wine on our table, my mother said, "What do you say we shoot some pool?"

I was excited. I'd played pool a couple times at an arcade. My mother was pretty good. She'd get up on her tiptoes and lean way over and squint her eyes and say "watch this" and, most times, make a shot. She beat me, and we shook hands, and while we were shaking, this guy came up, wearing a dark green woolly shirt and one of those sleeping-bag-type vests and cowboy boots and Levis. And he was smiling. He slapped a quarter onto the edge of the pool table. And my mother smiled. "What do you say?" he said. She said, "What the hell!" He said his name was Todd, and she introduced me and herself. "Do you mind, honey?" she asked.

I said (as if I didn't know), "About what?" She said *if I play one game of pool with Todd.* I didn't like the idea, but I could see that she was in the mood, so I said *fine.*

They played. Todd was pretty good. He hit the cue ball hard, and it slammed into the other balls and moved them around. He and my mother talked. I didn't hear everything; I kind of walked around. They were talking theater and stuff. I knew names of a lot of plays, but they were talking about poems too, and books, and I didn't know those.

They played a second game. Todd's hair was curly and the same color as my mother's. My mother grabbed the carafe of wine and brought it near the pool table, and they both kept pouring glasses. My mother was laughing. Todd was kidding around. He used his pool cue and did a thing that I'm pretty sure was a monologue because my mother shrieked, "Ohmygod, I can't believe it! I can't believe I'm in Montana and people are doing *The Cherry Orchard!*"

"You're in Livingston," Todd said. "It's very different."

After they finished their second game, they put quarters in the jukebox and danced. Close. My mother looked like she might go to sleep and then maybe like she *was* asleep and Todd was carrying her. Being careful. But then I saw that she wasn't asleep because she was moving her hands on the very top of Todd's back.

Then they finished, and Todd brought her over to where I was eating corn chips. "Thanks for the loan," he said. "I appreciate it."

"What loan?" I said.

"He means me," my mother said.

I said I knew that.

She stared at him. He looked over and smiled. He looked a lot like the men in the pictures with the trout.

"Thank you, ma'am," he said to her.

"Thank *you*, sir," she said.

"She's a hell of a pool player," Todd said.

Back at The Red Dog, I did a sketch of Todd. I got his hair really well, and his eyes and his sarcastic smile. It was pretty good. While we were getting ready for bed, I asked my mother: did she *like* Todd. She didn't say anything. She was by the mirror, brushing her teeth and just looking in and in. When I asked again, after we were in our beds, she just said, "You'd like a father, you'd like having a father, wouldn't you?"

I said I didn't care; it didn't matter. I could have a father or *not* have a father—it was all the same.

She said, "You don't mean that."

I didn't know what to say next. So I asked her again *did she like Todd?*

"I'm six years older," she said. "I'm twenty-nine, honey. He's twenty-three. But he was certainly nice." Then we fell asleep. I woke up in the middle of the night, and she was out of bed, the thin curtain at the window wrapped around her, and just staring out. I don't know why, but I didn't move; I stayed still.

We cut down into Yellowstone Park along U.S. 89. The sky was like a lake. When we got near the park, I saw smoke. "It's still the fire!" I said, but my mother said she didn't think so because the smoke was white not black, and was probably steam. "Geysers," she said. And it was. They were all over. And smaller things with colored moss and water that they called *paint pots.* We saw elk and bison and deer and huge birds. We got out of our car and walked down a hill to where the fire had been and walked into it—the black trees, the black grass—but not all of the trees were burnt: there was green. And flowers. "So they were right," my mother said.

"Who was right?" I asked.

"The people who said *don't do anything,*" she said.

"What people?"

"The people who said *don't interfere.*" And she reached her hands out and grabbed the trunk of a burned tree and twisted them, the way you do sometimes on a bat, and then took her hands with the black on them and rubbed them all over her face so she looked like a coal miner. "Next year, I'll be blooming again," she said. "And even better! It's not a problem."

We got onto U.S. 20 and crossed into Idaho. It was afternoon, and my mother was really quiet. I watched her forehead, which still had black on it, and her eyes. They were going through something. "Do you want me to change the tape?" I said around Big Springs, and she said, "What tape?" She started drumming her fingers on the steering wheel. We were by a town on the Snake River called Last Chance when she said, "Well, I guess it's time," and pulled in by what was called a fly shop, where there was a phone booth, and got out and placed a call.

"Were you calling B. Mitchell?" I asked when she got back in and we were going and passing a place called Harriman Ranch.

“His name is Buddy,” my mother said. “Buddy.”

“Were you calling Buddy Mitchell?” I asked.

“Yes,” she said.

“What did he say?”

“He said he was looking forward to...”

“What?” I said.

“I don’t know,” she said.

“He just said that he was *looking forward to*?”

“*Getting acquainted.* Something like that,” she said. Her voice sounded irritated—and she knew it, because then she said, “Honey, I’m sorry.”

I said, “Are you going to wash your face first?”

We went by Sugar City. And Rexburg. And Idaho Falls. There were rocks everywhere from volcanoes and, in one place, water that shot out of a cliff. I tried to get my mother to do monologues, but she wouldn’t. We went to Arco and then Carey and then Bellevue. It got dark. We went to Hailey and Ketchum, and my mother finally said something. She said, “Can you believe all these condominiums?”

“Are we ahead of or behind time?” I said.

She looked at her watch. “I guess a little ahead.” Then she said, “Can you last one more hour?”

“For what?” I said.

“For supper.”

I said sure.

We climbed up mountains, and they were pretty steep. “These are the Sawtooths,” my mother said. “This is called Galena Summit.”

“I know,” I said. “I’ve got the map.”

We headed down again. And it was a huge valley. Even though it was night, you could see. Because the moon was full. And the whole valley lit up blue, with the tops of the Sawtooths white and you could see why they called them the Sawtooths.

“This is pretty amazing,” my mother said.

“It is,” I agreed. And it was.

When we got to Stanley, just before Sunbeam Springs, it was almost nine, and the one place open for food belonged to Elvis Presley's drummer. That's what the man where we filled up on gas said. "Then," he said. "Not now. Now he's dead. Elvis, not the drummer."

I had a cheeseburger. My mother just had a beer: she said she wasn't hungry. The place, Jack's, was huge, with a bar but practically no tables to eat at. Mostly it had space, which my mother called a dance floor, which was probably true, since a man and woman were dancing. My mother watched and sipped her beer. She only finished half. I've tasted better cheeseburgers, but the French fries were okay.

When we got back in the car, my mother sat, not moving.

"Aren't we going?" I said.

"It's thirteen miles," she said. "Thirteen miles, we're there."

"To B. Mitchell's house?" I said.

"There's a café," she said. "He's waiting."

"Does he know *I'm* here?" I asked.

My mother didn't say.

"Mom?"

"He does," she said. "He knows your name," she said. "And that you're along and that you're twelve."

The road to Sunbeam Springs went along the Salmon River. Coming around one bend, our headlights filled up with smoke. "Oh!" my mother said.

It was like the steam in Yellowstone. "Honey they're *hot* springs," she said. "From the mountain!" She was smiling, and I was glad. "Look! They go down to the river!" She turned the car onto a pull-off and jumped out. "Come on," she said. "Look!"

There was white steam everywhere—and the same smell we'd had that morning in the park. "God, this is amazing!" she said. "This is I mean, this is extraordinary. I can't believe this!"

Then she took my hand, and walked me down a path to where the hot spring water washed into the black river. People had put stones around and made pools. "I love this!" my mother yelled up into the sky. "I just want you to know, I love this!" And then she bent and dipped a hand into a pool. "Oh God," she said. "Oh, dear!" And then she got what-she-calls-when-I-get-it *antsy.* She got antsy and began wriggling and saying, "I don't know, I don't know if I can resist this, it's asking a lot." And then she said, "Oh, hell, come on, you live once!" and then, "Are you with me?"

I wasn't sure. I wasn't sure what she was up to. I said, "With *what*?"

She said, "With me." Then smiled. "With *me,* with *me*. What do you say?

I said *all right.*

She said, "Just follow." And she pulled off her sneaks. And then her skirt. "It's an adventure," she said.

"I guess," I said. Though I still didn't know what it was she was planning.

It was cold. The wind came down the ravine where the river was, the way it sometimes blew down streets in Brooklyn. But I took my sneaks off. Then my pants. My mother was completely naked now and stepping into one of the pools and making sounds like a bird. Pretty soon I was in a different pool, close beside her, and it felt weird—I have to say that—it felt weird at first, a little weird. I felt uncomfortable to be naked outside in a river with my mother.

"Spectacular!" she yelled out at the sky. "Spectacular!"

"Spectacular!" I yelled. It seemed the thing to do.

"Spectacular!" she yelled again, and then we yelled "Spectacular!" together. I felt better.

She was pretty. I have to say that. She was pretty, and the moon was full, and the water felt just amazing—hot, then cold—perfect. And my mother's skin—I shouldn't have looked at it, probably, but I did. I couldn't stop—it was pink. All the black from the Yellowstone fire had been washed away from her face. "You know, if it's just this," she said. "If it's only this it's okay."

We dressed. We didn't have towels, but the wind dried us. It was icy cold. But it didn't feel bad. It didn't feel bad at all; the steam was nice. Then we climbed back to the car and started up.

Two miles later, we saw the Sunbeam Springs Café. It was lit. And as we got close, I could see a man sitting by the window, wearing a red hunting cap, and I could hear my mother pull in her breath. She saw him too.

He got bigger but not big. He was looking through the glass. He wasn't young. He had marks on his face. My mother drove past and didn't pull in. She drove about a half mile and didn't talk. I knew I should keep quiet too. When she pulled over, the car still running, I waited for her; I knew she wouldn't want me asking before she said. She put her hands together and hit the tips of her fingers against her lips and started shaking her head.

"I..." Something happened to her next words.

"What?"

"I can't do it," she said.

I knew what she meant, and knew she meant it.

We sat there together a while. Then she reached for her door handle. "I'll just be a minute," she said. "I need to breathe some of this air again. You stay here." And she opened her door and got out and walked in front of the car where I could see her in the lights, and she put her head back so it was faced way up into where the stars were. And the moon. And I could see her breathing—big breaths—then letting them out, her breath like what had gone up out of the hot springs.

When she came back, she said, "Will you be angry?" And I said, "No. But I have to go to the bathroom." And she said, "I'll pull over onto the blind side of the café and you can go in."

And she did that. And I went in. And B. Mitchell still was sitting by the window and looking out. He had on a black shirt and yellow tie. I think he'd sprayed his hair. He looked okay. Not bad. He didn't look as old as he had driving past, but—but he was a lot older than my mother. And his face was one of those faces: my mother says they're people who've had complexion problems when they were young.

I asked the man behind the counter where the restroom was. B. Mitchell heard me and he turned and looked. The counterman pointed down a hall. Now B. Mitchell was pressing his face hard against the glass and had a hand up to one side to help him see into the night.

I peed. I came out. B. Mitchell was there again and looked at me. I looked back. He nodded. I nodded. He looked like a nice person. He looked like a person who might be fun and might take you on a fishing trip or on a hike or on a horse somewhere. He sort of gave me a smile. He had friendly teeth. But he wasn't young.

He said *evening*. I said *evening*. He said *how're you?* And smiled. I didn't say anything back. His voice came real deep and quiet, like a voice that I wouldn't've minded if—at the end of a day—it came through a door. Except it wouldn't.

Because he was just a guy. Just an older guy. Just a guy who I can still draw, a year after. A guy with a bumpy face and a black shirt and a yellow tie, sitting in a café by the Salmon River drinking coffee, waiting, staring through a window. Just a man with friendly teeth and sticky stuff on his hair who might have been my father.

THE BURNING LAKE

I confess: I can be a smartass. My mouth gets me in trouble. Most of my Sawtooth Regional AP students think it's cool—when I'm genuinely over the top, I own it. Although, when there's a smug, pushy parent...

Example: It's past midnight. There are dinner leftovers and a sense of argument in the room. My lover, Krista, is upstairs; I'm alone. The attorney-father's voice lingers on my skin like eczema. His complaint: I'd failed his son's *Gulag Archipelago* book presentation. Hey, his son, Aaron, hadn't known the meaning of either *gulag* or *archipelago.*

"So, you don't think Solzhenitsyn's ambitious?" the attorney-father'd said. "For a seventeen-year-old?"

"Sir," I'd said. "Solzhenitsyn's ambitious for a *thirty*-year-old. But—" Upstairs, I heard Krista running water.

The attorney-father'd listed Aaron's four AP classes, invoked achievements in both tennis and cross-country. *Plus debate!* he'd said. *Plus Features Editor!* Evidence! On to summation.

During summation, I'd inventoried the leftover coconut shrimp, black beans, and yellow rice.

This is a bright student, the attorney-father'd ended. *You've shut down a bright, motivated student. Are you proud?*

Some say I have an authority problem. It's possible. Certainly, I'm bad company for a bully. I told the father-attorney that students should know words they use. We went back and forth. I got hungry again. Stress makes me eat. Then, after I eat, I run. A lot of stress means a lot of eating and running. I don't gain weight.

The father-attorney'd accused me of wanting to fail his son.

I'd said, look—I'm not into failure; failure is the last thing I'm interested in. I'm at school late and arrive early. I invite students to my house. We build things, create magazines, make films. We did an *Old Man and the Sea* installation in the school cafeteria. I don't *fail* anybody. If students *fail*, they *fail* themselves. Aaron, I said, had had the class for two months—during which time, he'd not appeared for a single extra-credit book project. I was stretching for another coconut shrimp when the father-attorney'd cut to his chase.

"So what are you trying to fill these kids up with, anyway?" he'd asked.

I'd considered *helium* as an answer but rejected it and just answered. *What did I want? From my students? Okay:* "To develop an appetite for the impossible," I'd said.

The father coughed, then stalled. "Excuse me?"

I wasn't going to repeat myself.

"Excuse me? *Develop*? You call yourself a teacher!" he said—and hung up.

I'd set the phone down—slowly, precisely—feeling the father-attorney's fading words hover like industrial smoke. Upstairs, I could hear Krista move—here first, then there. Had she felt sent away, I wondered, or had she simply opted for distance?

I lack certain skills with women. Krista came into my life underwater. We'd swum toward one another, scuba diving in Florida—Islamorada. She'd been a double major—art and psychology at Sarah Lawrence. The night we met, we slept together. Krista's work involves print layout for magazines like *Elle* and *Vanity Fair* and *Mirabella*. She'll be turning thirty next month. I'm thirty-six.

Another confession: I've been teaching only six years. Before, I did three as a legislative reporter for an ABC affiliate in Albuquerque; before that, two as a fact-checker for *The Atlantic Monthly*. Also, there was a year each of learning the brokerage business at Morgan Stanley, writing copy for a small ad agency, and playing keyboard in an Irish rock band, The Aran Isles. My high school yearbook, *The Beacon*, invented a Senior Honor for me: *Michael Sanders—Most Restless.*

And that's fine; I own my restlessness. That said—I love teaching. Before teaching, most things I tried turned to wheel-spinning or failure. Or maybe they were all mentoring preparation, and I just didn't see it. At one point, I started a novel about an American painter in the Balkans. I don't paint. I'm not Balkan. Teaching, unquestionably, has upstaged the novel.

So, my night: attorney-father call; leftovers on the table; it's late. I stand at the foot of the stairs, and try a *hey*, wait, then follow it with a *Krista*. My voice can't hide itself; it's uncertain. It sweeps the dark above me, like a rag, an audible Swiffer.

Later, in the black hours of the night, I have a dream. In it, all the kokanee have returned to Redfish Lake, and there are silver wolves everywhere—content to be living with stately longhorns and pumas with manes. In this dream, just beyond where I stand—on a mesa— spotted hyenas in tuxes are doing stand-up comedy. So it's a happy dream—giddy, almost.

It seems I've taken a class of students up to Redfish, where I've chosen the most timid-yet-graceful in the lot, Allie McFadden, and invited her to walk across one of the inlets on the backs of the kokanee—a feat she accomplishes with exceptional grace and to the great appreciation of the class. It's a wonderful dream—the kind you wait for. A keeper.

The next day, my principal, Charlie Teamens, pulls me aside after Junior AP and concedes—okay, sometimes I'm quick and funny. But today he's not amused. "Come by at two," he says.

I remind him: Tuesdays after school are when kids bring in television-episode clips and make the case—using whatever book—that most of TV's been stolen from the Great Works. My first obligation's always to my students, I tell Charlie.

He says my obligation's admirable, but we have a father with Board of Ed. history. And he rehearses my attorney-father's grievances: (1) the evolution chapter in an elementary science book, (2) an abridged *Modest Proposal* in an eighth-grade anthology, (3) an American History text's take on Little Bighorn. What his kid reads, *he* reads, Charlie finishes. He pleads, "Let Aaron Borchers give his book report," and asks that I save him from another incident like my Huck Finn raft project out at Blue Heron Lake, where I had two students not go home but, instead, *light out for the territory*.

I smile. "Robbie Jacobsen and Mindy Fritz," I remember. "Great kids."

"Michael—you have authority problems," he says. Then, "Don't create an incident."

That night, in bed—after red meat for the first time in two months, then running fifteen miles, then lovemaking—I go off on a tear to Krista, who stops me, mid-sentence, saying I'm too intense. "Baby, chill," she says.

I remind her that, with sex, she *likes* intensity. "You direct it, in fact," I say.

Krista says, half the time, she feels I'm grading her when we have sex.

I tell her, *Of course!* And, *Always an A- or a B+*. I ask, *Are there any more of the garlic Stilton mashed potatoes left?*

The next day, Aaron's there with a ball-penned smirk pummeled on his face. "Something you ate?" I ask him. Later, Charlie Teamens pulls me aside again to say that a meeting's been scheduled at the district office. "My hope," Charlie says, "was to spare all of us this."

"Bring it on!" I crow. Charlie misses the humor.

"Have you any idea," he asks, "what this could possibly cost?"

I suggest that Aaron's father come to class. "Let him watch me teach," I say.

Charlie says he's ahead of me; he's done that, and Aaron's father, Peter Borchers, confesses no desire to watch me *perform*.

At home, Krista presses: "Michael, why do you always need to play the bad boy?" I tell her it's because I'm a Contra, and do a little Contra dance.

Krista splits for bed, but I'm not tired. I review my next-day preparations, then assemble a cherry almond coffee cake for the morning. By the time I get upstairs, Krista's taken all of our pillows.

The next day, a three-page, stapled manuscript, Aaron's Gulag, is sitting on my desk. The paper reads like CliffsNotes—patchwork internet paragraphs, Solzhenitsyn's biography, plot summary. The first sentence gives a definition of *gulag*; the second, of *archipelago*. I scribble *Too Late* at the top and set the paper aside.

Later, Charlie Teamens makes yet another appearance at my door. "You get the boy's report?" he asks. "His father called—said he'd left it."

I take a breath. I don't want to be contentious, but, "Charlie," I begin. I do the term-grade math. "It's the difference between an A and an A-," I explain. "It's one term. Of four!"

Charlie makes a kind of leveling gesture, spreading his hands. He says perhaps I've misunderstood; it's gone beyond *request*. "Give Aaron Borchers the credit," he says. "End of discussion."

That night, I'm making a bay scallop and lemongrass risotto and the television rocks me with news of a former student's murder. *Blake Henry executed by...* In my second year, Blake Henry had appeared in my AP. Brilliant. Passionate. Idealistic. Gifted—especially as a painter, but inspired in literature. He'd gone to Berkeley, but we'd continued our contact. After Berkeley, he'd gotten a full ride to the Chicago Art Institute, where painting had become political. When he'd graduated, only a year and a half ago, he'd gone to Bogotá, Columbia, working with a group calling themselves Food & Art For Democracy.

The news announces that Blake had personally organized a group of young students to paint an apartment complex mural picturing clearly identifiable drug lord faces. The heads of Blake and another student had been found at the site—faces splattered with paint.

I can't help it: I scream. I throw wooden spoonfuls of hot risotto against the walls. I claw and claw my face until it bleeds; I weep. When Krista walks in, she finds me sitting in the middle of the living room with a half-finished bottle of Stoli vodka. "Jesus Christ, Sanders!" she says. "What's going on? What's happened?"

I tell her.

"Oh, Jesus—fuck me!" she says. "Why do you have to take things so personally?" She leaves the room. I can hear her hanging up her coat, climbing the stairs, running water for a bath. I pursue.

"Look, I'm sorry," I say. "I'm sorry that I *take things personally*. But—!" It's hard to think of where to go after the *but*. "But that's the way I *am*."

"Right. Which is what I'm learning," she says, stepping out of her skirt.

When I put my hands on her shoulders, she shakes them away. "Krista, he had so much *life*," I try. "This boy—this young man! He had so much *life*. And *vision*. He was never afraid."

"Rules to live by," Krista says and walks by me, naked now, to her bath.

An hour later, out of a silence and over our badly salvaged risotto, Krista tells me she was late tonight because she's had an abortion.

I push clotted air out of my mouth. "Mine?" I ask.

"I'm not sure," Krista confesses, then reaches for the Stoli. She wipes the mouth of the bottle and slams some down.

We go to bed back to back.

Two days after I suggest Krista pack and leave, I attend a meeting at the district office—myself, Charlie Teamens, Peter Borchers, and the district's assistant superintendent, a Carla Russell, who begins almost every sentence with, "Well, though I'm only second in command, I know I speak for..." Peter Borchers—who's a sort of John Ashcroft lookalike—outlines his complaint. When he's done, the eyes in the room turn to me.

Questions of fact are debated, elaborated. The father says the reason Aaron hasn't joined any extracurricular class activities is *certain questionable rumors* about me circulate among the students. I warn him about defamation law. He laughs. At the end, Carla Russell, speaking (she's sure) for the Superintendent, declares, "In the case before us, I'm compelled to find the instructor's policies—though demanding and admirable—"

"High," I insert.

"Unacceptable and unreasonable," Carla Russell finishes.

I want to say, *kiss my ass!* Instead I say, "Okay, my expectations are *demanding*—but they're not *unreasonable*."

I'm told to change the grade—or suffer consequences. The father smiles. Charlie Teamens drops his head into his hand, where it rests like a football on a kicking tee.

I go home, change clothes, and run. I consider calling a friend at *The New York Times*, asking whether he wants an Op-Ed Education piece. The late afternoon's the color of fish bellies—white, grey, vaguely scaled. After running, I shower. In our bedroom, Krista's clothes and luggage are all over the floor, but she's nowhere.

Quieted by the run and shower, I dress and go to a memorial for my murdered student, Blake Henry. Perhaps a dozen classmates of Blake's are there. "Hey—Mr. S!" they greet. I remember them all—names, papers they'd written, comments in class. I rehearse my memories. We hug and laugh. They had been fine, bright kids, now grown into fine, young adults.

The memorial itself breaks my heart. There are candles—dozens. And, placed around the space, are drawings and watercolors Blake had given to his friends. A young woman, Janie, remembers Blake called them *beautiful exercises.*

And, of course, there's food. Lots—and I eat too much. Blake's parents are remarkably calm and generous. They circulate, holding close, tender, personal conversations. And then there are the videos Blake had sent home from Columbia—one so recent as to depict Blake and the Columbian students blocking out their mural on the exterior of the apartment wall. It's sad; it's brutal; it's heroic. I feel, at once, privileged and awash in a futile present world. Still, when I say goodbyes, I understand why it is I teach.

Outside, in the small Lutheran church lot and Idaho dark, I shake. I think, briefly, I will rage, but I don't. The night feels like night in another country—one miles and oceans away: dark, rubbled, riddled with inaccessible language. I feel alien, archeological. *Christ, where am I? Who? I need...need to move,* I think. But where? Krista's probably at home packing. Worse, she may be waiting to have a *serious* conversation.

My mind spits a kind of alum and bitterness. It growls vulgarities. Krista's and my first year was extraordinary. We scared each other, shared dreams, spent a week in Utah's Escalante wilderness, riding a full moon up into the sky on peyote. We mapped out a collaboration—Krista, the photographs; me, the text. Facing pages: alcoholic American Indians on one side, tribal casinos on the other.

It has to be relentless! I'd said.

Because you're relentless? she'd said and kissed me hard.

I feel crazy and restless. And—Jesus, even with all I'd eaten at the memorial—starved. Instead of heading home, I drive to a tavern—Deuces Wild. When I pull in, neon—blinking pink and turquoise—scatters the lot then collapses. Through the tavern windows, then out over the lot cinders, drifts the music of a small country band with ragged amplifiers.

Inside, the meager air, stagnant with smoke and bad weed, gives me pause—but not pause enough, so I find a small, remote table. I don't want conversation—just to drink. And although I don't drink whiskey, I order Maker's Mark, which—when it comes—tastes just as I'd hoped—like a fist to the mouth, coating my teeth, ripping at the back of my throat.

Couples dance. Women dance alone. A football game flickers on the bar's flat, oversized television. *Is it still football season?* A thin woman in an unbuttoned, pearl-buttoned cowboy shirt and Levis snakes an inspecting walk by my table. She's popping an index finger in and out of the mouth of an Old Milwaukee bottle, and she smiles. I do my best to respond.

"So was that a smile? Am I getting a smile from you?" The woman stops.

"Hard to say," I manage.

"Promises," the woman says. "Promises, promises," and moves on.

When two State Highway Patrol troopers walk in, the whole tavern—including the over-amplified band and television—gets quieter. The troopers stand, like oversized salt and pepper shakers, at the near end of the bar. The larger one starts roving, leaving the other as sentry.

I watch the rover stop by a succession of tables. He looks to be checking IDs, except the drinkers are all clearly of age.

He drifts until he stands beside my table. He expects me to do something. He lifts his head, studies the ceiling. When he lowers it, there's a smirk on his face.

"Something I can help you with?" I ask. I can't help it.

"Why don't you tell me," the trooper says.

Fuck you, I think, but hold it. I lift my glass and move some Maker's Mark into then around in my mouth.

"I'd like to see your license and registration," the trooper says.

"Because I was exceeding the speed limit?" I ask.

"I'd like to see your license and registration," he repeats. "And—in the event it matters—I don't have a lot of patience tonight."

"Hey, me either," I say. "Possibly it's contagious."

I see the trooper's left hand, where it rubs his left leg.

I remind him of the law. "The law is," I say, "you have to give reason for requesting. License and registration, I mean."

"That so. Well, then, fuck the law," the trooper says. "So you're a lawyer?"

"Judge," I say. "Judge. State Supreme Court."

The trooper holds position and eyes me. I watch his jaw flex in the kind of tension that can explode and leave bone shards and teeth scattered. Instead, he takes a deep breath and unmoors, moves. I watch, swilling the Maker's Mark in my mouth like a rinse, like a mouthwash, then swallow it.

Who knows? Maybe someone will discover *my* severed head on some nearby roadside tomorrow morning. *What a fascist world*, I think. There's a new power afoot, and it's the mood of the whole country; it doesn't make any difference *where* you live. Bosnia, Baghdad, Ramallah, Beirut, Tehran, Bogotá. Burley, Idaho! *Nobody likes people who are overqualified—especially if they're restless smartasses.*

The troopers leave. I walk to a window and watch them recede in their state car. "So, what was that all about?" I ask a bartender.

"They say they're looking for terrorists," the bartender says.

"Excuse me?" I ask.

"Terrorists," the bartender says.

"I see," I say. "I see. I should have figured it out."

The bar's customers have gone back to dancing. I pace, nurse my drink, leave. A notion's come into my head. It's about pedagogy and justice.

Outside, the night tastes like paraffin. It seems lit by more moon than the meek wafer in the sky and is hazed with a strange kind of dust. At some distance, I hear the wails of emergency vehicles.

I get into my Honda and begin the ride home. I'm somewhere, I know, in the hour before midnight. Willie Nelson is singing "Home Motel" on my radio.

A couple of miles from the Deuces Wild, the keen of fire trucks closes behind me then passes. The bartender's earlier answer echoes in my head: *Terrorists.* I think, *Well, if they could be in flight-simulation schools in Florida, they could be anywhere: Lincoln, Nebraska. Cody, Wyoming. Stanley, Idaho. Why not?* Now Willie Nelson is singing "I've Just Destroyed the World."

Abruptly, I see shimmering light. Miles ahead and slightly north, a kind of radical light pulses on the horizon. And there's a thin film forming on my car windshield—dust, pollen, ash. I roll the window, and there's the scent again, stronger, of hydrocarbon.

I betray my intent to go home and, instead, follow the wailing engines and hunt the expanding light—all of which turns me onto an off-road for Blue Heron Lake—one I know to be rough, so I drive with caution, trying to stay alert to ruts and dips—the air now salt-and-pepper almost, oily, black, flashing, like the sheen of a starling.

At every rise, each turn, it seems, the horizon brightens—until, from a crest, I see Blue Heron Lake burning. Flames eat the lake; the lake devours the fire. The whole lake's incendiary—shoreline to center.

I pull off onto a rough-grown thatch, cut the engine, step out. Just ahead and below, are eight hose-and-ladder trucks. Spumes of foam arch and fall onto the flames. *How can a lake burn?* I wonder. Perhaps it's the Maker's Mark. Maybe the whole day's been a dream. *How can a lake burn?*

In and around the trucks and spumes, voices bark—angry, argumentative. Behind me, another truck wails and clamors, nears, passes, and then descends.

I watch. *Terrorists. Terrorists*, I keep thinking—then I hike down to the trucks. Men in black oilskins are everywhere. Maybe a third of them wear gasmasks. And there seems to be an almost contagious anger: no one—as I read the dispute—is doing his job correctly. Everyone's in error. And still Blue Heron Lake burns; still spumes rain on its burning. If anything, the already wide swath of fire appears to spread.

A fireman on foot passes, moving back to secure something from a truck. "So, what happened?" I ask.

"No one knows." The fireman disappears behind his truck, reappears with a large tank strapped to his back, passes again. "Quick advice: If I were you, I'd get the hell out of here," he says. And moves on.

I watch him stride. The fire on the lake is lime green, then turquoise—an edible fire taken over by a poisonous one. I recall my Huck Finn class project and suddenly imagine a raft full of Twain-stricken adolescents—their lashed-together logs flaming.

The firefighters change the arc of their plumes and, over them, I can hear the sound of distant rotors. *They'll be dropping something*, I think, then stand and turn, walk back, turn the Honda key, and drive off.

Why would a lake burn? I think all the way home. *Ladybug, ladybug*! And, *I hope she's gone.*

She is—though there's residue everywhere, especially in the bathroom. It seems she'd used some twenty-percent criterion—any cosmetic, prescription, gel, paste with only twenty percent or less in it has been left. As well as a beaten pair of running shoes. And two tees—one with *Mind* printed over the left breast, *Body* over the right. It's a tee I'd given her, which, at the time, she'd thought funny.

Any books I'd given, she's left. She's taken all of hers and half my CDs. All my good pinots and cabernets are gone. And my cordless drill. She's left a yellow Patagonia vest—an error of her hurry, certainly. She loves the vest. Maybe she'll sneak back, when I'm at school, and nab it.

I try the television for late news. But it's over. News of the fire will have to wait until morning. The day's stretched me beyond tired and sore, so I work some of Krista's left-behind aloe into my shoulders and wrists. I can smell her in it. *Who—in her off hours—has she been fucking?* I wonder. *How does a lake burn?*

When I check, my machine has three messages. The first's from Charlie Teamens. He needs me at work an hour early *to get this whole over-inflated thing put to bed.* The second begins with dead air followed by an adolescent voice trying to disguise itself. *You're dead meat—you pathetic sack of shit*, it announces. Behind the adolescent voice, other muted adolescent voices laugh.

The third message is from Krista. *You want to know why I found someone else? Because more and more, you made me feel like an underachiever. Or overachiever. I can never remember which is which.*

I breathe in, breathe out, shake my head. Images of Blake Henry's parents, then Blake in a watercolor self-portrait swim into my head. My jaw shakes, and I jam my tongue against my lips. I feel so hungry…and angry…and sad.

It's late—*late*, but I can't sleep. So I position myself at my PC. I've had an idea and, right or wrong, I need to follow it through.

I compose a document—a simple, single page with *agrees-to* and *in-return-agrees-to* terms. At the bottom, I create signing spaces for both Aaron Borchers and myself. When I'm done, the house seems hollow. The heat ducts and electrical conduits surge and shuffle with insomnia. I fight for sleep.

In the morning, the local front-page photo of the burning lake calls its cause *undetermined.* There are theories: a lumber firm stopped from clear-cutting nearby; a power company wanting to dam the lake for a reservoir; a tribe refused casino-building rights on the shore.

I go early and swing into Charlie's office. I announce his troubles are over. "Kid gets his A," I say. Then, just as fast, I disappear. "Shouldn't we talk about this?" I hear, fading, behind me.

I pull Aaron aside before class. I hand him a contract. The exchange is simple. I'll give him his A for the remaining year—all terms, all assignments. In return, he agrees to: (1) always attend, (2) do no work, (3) never participate. He looks confused and apprehensive. "I don't get it," he says.

"Right, exactly," I smile. I push the paper forward, point, hand him a pen. "The line above where it says *Aaron Borchers,*" I suggest.

He's cautious. We go back and forth. *What's the trick? No trick. Why are you doing this? It seemed logical.* Finally, given my name's already on and I've dated the document, Aaron shrugs and signs.

I extend my hand; he takes it. "See you tomorrow," I say.

The next day involves a discussion of *The Great Gatsby.* At one point, I hoist my personal copy. "First edition," I announce. "Valuable. Gift to the first student who can give me, specifically, the dimensions of Dr. T. J. Eckleburg's retina."

At first, there's a collective pause. Cathy Eagan raises her hand, but when I call on her, she gives the billboard size, not the retina. I look theatrically glum, shake my head.

Again, I hold the first edition high—at which point the girl of my dreams, the fish-walker, Allie McFadden, volunteers. "Allie!" I say, and she knows, and I present her the book. The bell rings. Aaron Borchers is the last student from the room.

I can see he's processing. "Aaron?" I say.

But he just shakes his head and leaves.

The next day—we're still on *Gatsby*—I extend my left arm, making my coat sleeve ride up and reveal my watch. "Rolex!" I hurl. "Who wants a Rolex?" I pull it off. "First student to recite—keep your books closed!—the remarkable final sentence of this book gets this Rolex."

A single hand rises. Daniel Hagar's.

"Daniel?" I prompt, then dramatically stretch my hands out as to receive a gift, which Daniel dutifully gives, reciting: "So we beat on, boats against the current, borne back ceaselessly into the past."

"Excellent!" I say. "Excellent, Daniel!" And I extend my Rolex.

Leaving the building that day, Charlie Teamens catches up. "I'm hearing rumors," he says. Seven smartass comebacks spin the Rolodex of my mind. I leave them there.

"Nice tie," I say.

On the third and final *Gatsby* discussion day, when I enter, every student's nose-deep in text. Several have CliffsNotes. "Hello! Good morning!" I say, and sense something inside me is either desolate or buoyant. I try to disregard the snake in the treasure chest, push through for a cavalier smile, and set the class in motion.

Today's about vision imagery. We discuss class structure through the lens of capitalism. With each new turn, Aaron Borchers' hand makes a vacant froth of the air. I ignore him. His face takes on the look of a battered child. My plan is, at about forty minutes in, I will remove my wallet and—laying them down carefully on his desk—withdraw five one-hundred-dollar bills.

"So, today's question," I begin. "Okay, books shut, notes put away—for a scholarship award of five hundred dollars."

Silence freezes. I inventory the faces. I see ferocity. I see need. I see competition. *Jesus Christ.* What have I set in motion?

Aaron's hand's already up, and I can see sweat. "Me! Choose *me*," he says.

I hold my dog-eared Fitzgerald text out like a church offering plate.

"Whatever you're going to ask—I know it!" Aaron says. At least a half-dozen other faces are as eager.

Something like a dust devil has its way with my brain. I imagine I'm in the Escalante Wilderness. On my tongue, on the roof of my mouth, I can taste Krista. "Listen—I'm sorry," I say. "I don't know what else to say…I don't know how else to explain it. I'm sorry."

After school, I run. All afternoon. Run and run. I wonder if I might be coming down with something. I've stocked my refrigerator with paella-makings—clams, chorizo, shrimp, chicken. The air in the distance is clearing. There's less ash—less smell of citronella and oil lamps. The cause of the fire still hasn't been determined. If there are terrorists, none of them have been found.

My lungs burn and swim. What had seemed pungent irony at first—forcing a public goat-dance from Aaron Borchers—now feels distastefully small, small and vengeful, and it makes me ashamed. And *Jesus—Jesus-fucking-Christ, I feel hungry!*

I imagine my running to be directionless—but it isn't. The truth is, it's long distance with an intent. However the highway snakes, it's still the highway—the same highway which leads off eventually north, to Blue Heron Lake.

When I get to the lake road, I angle onto it. I feel starved. My running shoes turn on loose rocks, beating the October dust into the twilight air. Overhead, a pair of osprey seems confused. I descend a hill, and the slapping of my shoes flush a half-dozen elk from a grassy meadow and toward trees. The air I suck grows increasingly sere and ammoniac.

When I reach the rise above the lake, it's almost dark—maybe ten, maybe fifteen minutes left. Still, there's enough light, and the lake is remarkable—an eye, a blue eye, but a blue eye with a scab. There appears to be an oval of ash irised in one sector.

I stop and look out. And what I see is like the negative of my fish-walking, stand-up hyena, *Peaceable Kingdom* dream—a scene almost primal-beyond-primal. Still, I descend to the lake's edge where there's a campground.

Something foul hovers: a smell, carnal and rank—more than ash, more than fire-retardant.

I spot a green campground litter drum from which—as I approach—the rankness rises. When I raise the drum lid to investigate, I almost choke. I guess moose. Maybe elk. Someone's shot and dressed a very, very large animal—and dumped the entrails. I set the lid back, move away, stumble to the edge of Blue Heron Lake, where I reflexively kneel, wash my hands, then my face.

Dead trout float everywhere. Nothing feels synchronous or harmonic here in this raw nightfall moment, especially myself. But then—maybe two hundred feet from where I kneel—I see a man surrounded by water, a figure hip-deep, *half* a man, really—equipped with waders, a vest, and a fly rod.

I rise and wander in the half-man's direction. For a while, I stand and watch as his line shoots back, shoots ahead—back and forth. The fly lands, drifts…lands, drifts. It's a lone fisherman's dumb-show. Perhaps a hundred dead cutthroat float on the chemically anointed surface—drifting there like troubled memories.

Finally I can't stand it. The burning lake's stolen the trouts' oxygen. They have no way to assume life, no way to glide into its current, take it in. Surely the half-man—as experienced a fisher as he appears—knows this.

"What are you doing?" I yell across the scabbed water, but he gives no indication of hearing. Instead, he shoots his line forward, back, forward, back, and places his fly. In my vision, his rod-hand, in the casting, seems uncannily phantom and disengaged. "What are you doing?" I call again.

"What does it look like I'm doing?" the man returns over his shoulder.

Smart as I believe myself to be, at this given moment I can't frame an answer.

"You fish?" the man calls.

"I have," I say. "I've made the attempt on occasion."

"Well—if you fish, then you know," the man calls.

"But they're all dead," I return. "They're dead. They're floating."

"Possibly," the man says, cocking his arm, looping his line forward, back. "Possibly. But, when it comes down to the wire—you know the wire?—when it comes down to the wire, you can't *not* fish." His fly hits the water. He raises his pole.

And—in the grim, bleak, falling and angry light—all my hunger and restlessness suddenly leave. What I feel instead is the vigilant, stark, sometimes even courageous dedication of fishermen, holding their places in bodies of water in the diminishing light.

BETWEEN PROJECTS

The first time Karen spotted the famous actor, he was in a red Pyranha Attak kayak, floating by her cabin on the Payette, rolling over—once, twice—before looping and paddling back out of sight upstream. She'd been throwing a large raku jar on her picnic table outside, letting her hands shape it, letting them center and guide her.

Something about the kayak, or roll, or actor—recognizable even helmeted, even at a hundred feet—broke her focus, and the raku bulged, lost itself, misshaped. Sometimes, she'd read, the actor hung out on the Big Wood. And, of course, he'd made his famous river movie. But that, she thought she remembered, had been in Montana. So, what was he doing this side of Galena, doing rollovers in a Pyranha? He was of The World. Karen was not. And she did not like The World's intrusion on her centering.

Again, he glided into her frame and, this time, waved. Karen gestured back and felt clumsy, childish. She unplugged her North Star portable wheel and went inside, where she stood—flushed and confused—in the rough, raw-wood, two-room space. Why was it so hard to live in refuge?

She could smell the cabin's pine pitch, taste something at once silical and ferrous. Something buzzed in her brain or blood, rattled her head, leaked down her arms and spine. There was no course to it. It was a nerve shiver.

What was a man like that doing on the Payette in Lowman, Idaho? Not that people couldn't go anywhere. They could. And did. Obviously. Retreat. Escape. *Karen* had. First from Sacramento. Then Boulder. Two years ago, from Boise. Life prompted, and you moved from and to. Life did whatever it chose to do to you, and you managed. Reconciled from Boise, it had been more inertia—continuing...who could say? Maybe the greater urge had been solitude. She'd used different explanations at different times, and in different months. At thirty-four, Karen was a once-soft woman, made wary living alone, making pots, shipping them to galleries in Boise and Ketchum, Vail and Colorado Springs, Santa Barbara—a woman living alone and supporting herself, which was no small thing.

She was not unattractive. Others said that; it was not her judgment. At five-ten, she was, okay, a bit tall, maybe more chunky recently, though her perhaps defensive vote would be *muscular*. She enjoyed eating. But that was fine; she walked five miles every day. Fished. She'd had a child once—*in a previous life*, which was what, when confessing, she confessed. The father'd been an older man, no one special, more a test than a passion. It hadn't been, truth told, that complicated—a time, a need, a boy-child. There were couples hungry for adoption. But, yes—a child. Somewhere in the year after her brief and failed convent experience. *Why did this famous actor in a kayak fluster her?*

He stood back from her block window and stared out. He was lost to the frame again. Would he float back? Was he caught in a pattern—a film loop of himself—until some splice took place? Wasn't that how they edited film?

She imagined him coming, at some point, onto her porch, knocking on her door—seasoned voice in a mantra greeting: *Hello? Hello?* He'd explain himself. He was renting the Jacobs' cabin half a mile upstream. Did she have any distilled water? Or, if it wasn't water, maybe he was out of sunblock—did she have some? He'd be heading to Stanley, to the Merc, tomorrow; he'd return it. Then he'd grow unnaturally shy, introduce himself. *That was dumb!* he'd say. *Guy knocks on your door, asks to borrow, acts like of course you know him when why should you? Mind if I step inside?*

Then—because she'd backed from the intimidating world too much, hadn't held her ground—*Sure, come in*, she'd say. Maybe say too loud. *Would you like a beer? How about some coffee—tea?*

Hey, he'd say. *Why not?*

She was close, probably. Near the mark. She'd seen his type, watched its intrusive certainty. Certainly imagined it. *Why not?* Yeah. He was a why not kind of guy.

They'd sit across her oak table, bottles or mugs between them. She'd be trying not to betray that, even though he looked older or thinner or shorter than she'd assumed, he—despite her semaphore of red flags—quickened her breath.

So, tell me. Tell me about yourself, he'd say.

And she'd, out of reflex, look down. Then up. *Not really that much*, she'd say, and rub the back of her knuckles nervously.

Oh, right. You say that, he'd say. *But there has to be.*

And she'd laugh. Nervously. Probably annoyingly. Then say, *Okay*. Start in. About her father and his various white-collar crimes. Rough out the whole business of her becoming a nun. Okay—not *becoming*. That actually was the point: *not*. Not becoming. About her summers spent fighting wildfires—first Montana, then here in Idaho. *The world blazes—I'm up to its heat*, she would let him know, in one way or another.

He'd nod—with emphasis when the narrative occasioned. Because she *had*, in fact, stories of consequence to tell. Of size. Nothing exactly tragic; still, for a kid growing up in an eleven-room house, on a Denver cul-de-sac called Estes Circle, she held her own. Even with a man like him.

Was he there still? On the water—*in* the water? No, didn't appear to be.

Maybe he was preparing for a movie scene—one with him chasing somebody in a kayak. And was getting the feel. Or who knew, perhaps the movie was happening, and she'd missed the cameras. She could be a bit tone-deaf (or color-blind) to local events. Oblivious. Lowman. Boise. She almost never read the

Wind River Journal. And Stanley didn't have enough news in its dust to have even a weekly. So if there were a film being shot, good luck to her knowing about it.

She took a long drink of her tea, which had lost its heat. Someone rapped the frame on her porch screen. She turned. It was the actor.

"Hey," he said. He raised his hand and smiled. He still wore his blue paddling jacket over a faded green tee. Khaki shorts. Akona sport shoes. Dark glasses. "Excuse me," he said.

"Oh—hello," Karen said.

"Sorry, but—" He reached, and she thought he was going to remove his glasses. Instead, he adjusted them. "I'm renting next door. Upstream. Jacobs' place. Got in last night, and staying a month or so. I went to make some tea—except the cabin doesn't have distilled water. And I thought maybe—" He smiled.

"Sure," Karen said.

"Could I borrow—? I'm going over to Stanley tomorrow. I'll bring some back from the mercantile."

Karen—trying to stifle anything eager—pushed the screen open. "Please," she said. "Come in. I'll get it. Is a gallon enough?"

"More than."

The actor moved himself into the space. "I saw you in the kayak," Karen said.

"Attak's a nice little boat," he said.

Karen lifted the gallon from her pantry floor, set it on her counter. "Would you like, I don't know, a beer? Some tea?"

"Tea's what I was going to make." The actor pointed to the jug.

"Happy to save you the trouble," Karen said, gesturing, indicating a second chair pulled up tight across from where she'd been sitting. The actor nodded, pulled the chair out, sat.

"I have green or black," Karen said.

"Green, please," the actor said.

Karen thought, *Okay, déjà vu*, lit the burner under her enamel pot, set about spooning some green tea into an aluminum ball. The actor introduced himself. "Yes. I recognized you," Karen said. "Nice to have you as a neighbor."

"I'm between projects," the actor said. "Finished one four months ago. Trying to figure out what to do next. Time on my hands. You do pots?"

"I do," Karen said. "Pots." It annoyed her when people called them *pots*. The tea water whistled. Karen cut the flame, lifted, poured steaming water into a smaller ceramic pot nearby. "This one's mine," she said. "My work. My *pot*. From when I first started."

"I like the glaze."

"Thank you. I'm into glazes."

The actor scanned the walls, where some of Karen's pottery equipment hung on hooks. He pointed. "There's a name for those things—but I can't remember it," he said.

"Extruders," Karen said. She carried the teapot to the table. "Give it a minute," she said. Then sat.

"Tell me about yourself," the actor said, and leaned his chair back. His teeth were perfect. His jaw was square. He had far more lines around his eyes than Karen would have guessed. "Tell me about yourself," he repeated.

Karen laughed.

"What?"

Spreading her hands, Karen fashioned a headline. "Famous Actor Makes Small Talk," she said. "Just like the rest of us."

The actor paused, lifted the lid, opened it, dipped the tea ball. "Looks good," he said. "You want some?"

"Sure, why not?" Karen said.

He poured hers, then his. "So you're choosing mystery," he said.

Karen focused beyond the window, on the river. She saw a trout rise. Was she choosing mystery? She saw two mink on the far bank, one of them slipping into the water. She knew the actor was waiting. She saw the possibility she was being impolite, partially enjoyed it, wondered if he would prompt again, but he only waited—once, twice sipping his tea. He took his time tasting it. Swallowed. *Oh, hell—why not?* she thought. *This is all imaginary anyway. Why not?*

And so she began. Her father. Then her mother. Talking about them as parents in two separate families—neither hers. She confessed the power, good and bad, of Catholicism. Speculated that, at heart, she was a submissive—at first religiously, then sexually. "Or maybe there isn't really a difference," she said. "Maybe *God* is just a word for disembodied sex. Or the other way around."

"So—I just want to be clear here—you're saying—?" The famous actor's face—*how did he do that?*—split down the middle: half serious, half confused. He grinned. "You're saying? The *God* thing?"

"I don't know. Like *Dog*—that anagram. Is it an anagram? I get confused. God-Dog: the same thing, backwards."

In part, she hoped the actor might see her as crazy, a recluse, a lunatic who had just traded a gallon of distilled water for an hour of prattle.

She went on about firefighting, spinning out theories connecting fire and hypnosis, unreeling all the folklore of human spontaneous combustion. *Go for it!* she thought. *So he's a famous actor. Fuck it. Why stop now?*

For the most part, the actor sat attentive; his sunglasses a reflective anthracite blue. He leaned forward in a possibly studied but engaged way. There were—not exactly nods—tics of his head at the right moments. Maybe this was a challenge to him—playing the part of an Absorbed Listener. It didn't matter. Faking it, not faking it. It was an hour's rush, her solo, and Karen hadn't had a solo in months. It was cathartic. She imagined two, three years from now, musing to a lover: *The last time I told this story was to...*

Finally, she hit what she thought the perfect high note—

something about the boy-child she'd birthed and given up—and held it. She imagined a gasp. The note lingered. She cut it off. *Finis!* The wind, Karen could hear, had picked up, moving over the Payette. It was almost whistling, certainly humming. Between herself and the actor, nothing disturbed the silence.

Until the actor pushed back, digging his heels into the wood floor, the two front legs of his chair hovering. "So," he began. "I'm interested in this, this father of yours—he's in prison now? Or out."

"Out," Karen said. "Out since last November. Somewhere."

The actor laughed. "I'm laughing because the industry word—I believe *wrong* industry word—is I can't play reprobates. Just rogues. So—I have to be honest here—your father interests me. He just arrives?" the actor asked. "Boom—from nowhere. No pattern, no announcement?"

"Oh, there's a pattern, I suppose," Karen laughed. *Is a rat's nest a pattern?* "Knuckles on the door—wherever. I go, I open it. *Hello, Kiddo.* And there he is! *You inviting me in?* What's my choice? I'd thought myself safe—I'd tried not to leave breadcrumbs."

"So he's wily."

"Oh—wily!"

"*I* could do wily. So then he stays? Mooches?"

Mooches seemed an odd word for the actor. "Mooches? No. Arrives always with money," Karen went on. "As in, *a lot.* Last time—over two hundred thousand. *Kiddo? You got a cookie jar? Flour tin I can store this in?*"

"Wild!" the actor said. He seemed buzzed.

"Yeah. Usually leaves five, ten, fifteen thousand behind. *Milk money,* he calls it. My father believes the law's for people who don't know what to do next, except with guidelines. So," Karen shrugged. Clearly, in telling her story, she had caught the actor's attention. One hand on either temple, he removed his sunglasses.

"You should write this up," he said. He pinched the bridge

of his nose, massaged his eyes, which were uncommonly blue. "Do a kind of a treatment. I could help." He set his glasses back carefully and stood. "Thanks for the tea," he said, then crossed to the plastic jug. "And for the water."

Was he staring? Hard to know. It seemed some sort of assessment was going on. The actor lifted the jug into the air like a trophy. "A loan," he announced, and moved to the door, swung it, stepped through, let it slap shut behind. "Thanks again."

"Hope it works out."

"And I meant what I said." The actor pointed a finger. "Write your life up."

That evening, after nine, he was back. "I shot my wad at the mercantile," he said. He carried two jugs of distilled water and a bottle of Cabernet. "I would have waited till morning, but I saw your light."

"I was cleaning my wheel."

"Well, we all need to clean our wheels, every once and again," he grinned. He raised the Cabernet. "This is yours—but I can't think of anything nicer than your inviting me in and the two of us sharing it."

Don't do this. Don't, Karen told herself. But she did. And *they* did—this time, Karen cross-examining the actor. *Why Lowman? Why the Payette?*

The actor lifted his chin, smiled enigmatically, and poured more wine. "I like places on water where there are attractive women with stories. Say more about your firefighting," he said. And Karen thought, *Firefighting, c'mon!* Then he shifted: "Tell me the two words that most define your life," he said.

Without a pause, Karen said, "Firefighting and passionfruit."

It was after midnight when he left. He leaned in and kissed Karen on the cheek. "Sorry. To presume. It's just—I enjoy you."

"I don't have a snappy answer," Karen said.

"We're still writing the script," the actor said. "I thought maybe I'd say what your father would say." And he vanished into the dark.

Early the next morning, he banked his Pyranha on a bed of rocks as she was firing her oval kiln. He set a hand on his green Deluge headgear. "You like trout?" he called. Karen confessed that she did. "I'll bring some by around five. You like Guinness?" Karen nodded. "Guinness and trout, then. Five." And he pushed the kayak from the bank with a paddle.

During the day, off and on, he'd drift into her frame, raise a paddle. She'd wave back. Something about him seemed unnaturally boyish—a quality which logic argued should be disarming but wasn't. She found a phrase forming in her head: *Men like that... Men like that...* She warned herself, *Don't finish the sentence.*

Instead, she threw two new pots—both raku jars. When two curious hikers stopped and watched, then asked, she said she was making orioles' nests. "For fish," she quipped. Something antic or angry was in her. "Orioles' nests for minnows." Minnows, she said, were hard to work into the clay. "In the end, though, it's worth it," she said. *Assholes*, she thought. Then reproved herself. *The world intrudes*, she thought. *The world stops by. It doesn't end. I need to learn that.*

The actor arrived punctually—a canvass creel over one shoulder, a six-pack of Guinness in his fist. "Evening, Fire Lady," he said. She'd been seasoning embers in her stone pit between glazing her oriole pots.

"These are ice-cold," he said, hoisting the six-pack. "Extra stout. You game?"

Karen dipped both her hands into her rain barrel, worked the grit off, and dried them on a towel. She took the dark, frosty bottle extended to her.

They drank and talked—somewhat against her better judgment. The actor grilled the trout. He'd brought lemon and dill, strips of bacon and oregano. His cooking skills were impressive. At one point, somewhere past nine, he took Karen's hair in his fist and pulled her to him. "Don't," she said.

"I'm sorry," he said. "It was an impulse."

"Yes, I could see," she said.

He seemed both regretful and astonished that she would resist. He kept tendering sentences which began, *I didn't mean to.* He knew he'd breached something and wanted to make his gaffe right, but Karen kept waving his words away.

"How sexual is your father?" he asked.

He was at her door just after sunrise the next morning. "I couldn't sleep," he said.

"I slept fine," she said. "No dreams. No waking up. Just sleep."

"How about I get to play host. You come over at noon. I'll fix lunch."

"I'm fine. I'm comfortable here," Karen said.

"You start putting down your life story? For me to show people?" If a shadow can be smug, a smug shadow drifted over the actor's face.

Give me a break! Life story! Karen thought. "I need to get to work," she said. "I promised my gallery in Santa Barbara I'd ship a dozen pots today. Why don't you do whatever it is you do—read scripts. I'll take a rain check."

"Rain check given," he said. "But at least—later, when you're ready to ship—let me drive you."

Why do men feel they need to volunteer doing things for women? "You know, I'm a terrific driver," Karen said. "I enjoy it."

"Are you refusing me?"

What Karen wanted to say was: *I'd like this day for myself.* Instead, she said, "Fine. Four. Be on time."

"Thank you, Fire Lady," the actor said. He smiled.

After they'd finished mailing, he'd not take no for an answer and insisted on treating Karen to drinks and dinner. It was the Stanley Kasino Club's happy hour and the bar was crowded, but the dining room was slow. Karen ordered a Crown Royal; the actor, a Maker's Mark. As soon as their server left, the actor leaned in. "I need your help," he said. "Badly. Your advice. Which project should I do next?"

Their drinks arrived; the actor raised his glass. "To the power of strangers," he said. "I really need a woman's counsel." And he outlined two possible acting projects and a directing project. The first project was a thriller. *Character-driven*. A political espionage film. He would play a CIA agent. The plot involved an assassination attempt on the president's wife. His character and the president's wife, in the process, fall in love. *Blah, blah, blah*. He liked doing political films. Maybe Karen had heard, at one point, he was considering candidacy. The other film was a romantic comedy. His first stage breakthrough had been comedy. He had a knack. "Or at least people *say* that," he said. Then added, "And, I think, with justification." He relished whimsy, he said. Spontaneity. Silliness. But life and career, in general, had taken him away. Had she seen—? He named a couple of romantic comedy roles he'd played. She'd seen one. Was he neglecting, did she think, a significant comic talent? "Or I could play a reprobate," he said. "Character like your father."

They took a break for their drinks.

The actor moved the Maker's Mark around with his tongue. He swallowed, nodded. "This is helping," he said. "Already." He smiled. "Of course, once you get your life written up for me, everything else goes on hold. I'm buying the rights. To play your father. But let me finish up."

The directing project, he said, was a kind of Aryan Nation against the Sierra Club thing, that would be shot in the Frank Church Wilderness, "which would have to be the most beautiful place in the world." He asked Karen whether she'd read he'd been a painter. *Sorry, no*, she said. She hadn't.

"They say I have a visual sense," he said. "They also say I'm a better director than an actor—which doesn't make me particularly happy."

"Why not?" Karen asked. Thought, *Christ, he's upset that—!*

"Because I'm supposed to be an actor."

People who need to see themselves as only one thing! Karen thought. "You can't be *both*?" she asked.

Their server returned with two new drinks on the house. She asked whether they'd had time to look over their menus, then recited the specials. "What should I have?" the actor asked. "The veal chops," Karen said, feeling the Crown Royal.

"The veal chops," the actor echoed.

"You are," the server began. "The owner said you *had* to be—"

"Don't do it," Karen advised. "Don't ask him."

"I'm sorry," the server said.

Karen ordered. The server left. The actor mulled, leaned in.

"I need you to tell me: what's your sense of me?" he asked.

"A man who borrows distilled water, listens to my stories, and grabs my hair," she said.

"I'm supposed to decide which project by October first."

"Do the directing project," Karen snapped.

The next day, the actor stopped by four times, asking whether she'd had any more thoughts. She hadn't; she'd been working, or trying to. The fourth drop-over, at seven in the evening, he carried a blackened grill laden with coconut shrimp.

"My specialty," he said. In his free hand he carried a bottle of Crown Royal, which he extended. Karen shook her head.

"I can only drink that stuff once every couple of months," she said.

"Share my shrimp," he said. He looked sad.

They sat outside, each with a Guinness. The sun lay behind the mountains; the sky, green; the river, mineral—mutton jade, opal and turquoise. "Is there a better place?" Karen asked.

"This reminds me of Australia," the actor said. "Do you know the Maori?"

Maori! Australia! Jesus! Name-dropper! "More, I'd say it reminds me of the Payette River in Lowman, Idaho," Karen said, and put her hands over her face, where she could smell the clay in them—the mud, the silicate, the oils and pigments from her glaze. And there was a trace-taste of flint, as well, from somewhere—maybe the kiln, maybe the wheel.

"So, are you thinking?" the actor asked.

"No, I'm smelling my hands," Karen said.

"Hey!" A man's voice boomed into the moment.

Karen ripped her hands from her face. "Oh, Jesus! God!" she said.

"Who? What?" the actor asked.

"Kiddo?" the voice boomed again.

Karen looked out, away—the actor watching.

"How do you get across this? Is there a bridge somewhere?"

On the far side, a man in a Levi's jacket stood carrying a black duffel. He had a thin-brimmed Stetson over his eyes.

Karen put a hand secretively to the side of her mouth. "Every two years," she said.

"Your father?"

Karen rolled her eyes.

"Amazing!" the actor said.

"Hey, how you doing, kiddo?" Karen's father called. "Am I interrupting something? Send the ferry across!"

"Sorry. The ferry's kaput. Walk back to the road! I'll come get you!"

The man tipped his hat, hoisted his duffel.

Karen stood.

"You want me to come?" the actor asked.

Famous actor as puppy dog, Karen thought. "It doesn't matter," she said.

"Why don't I come?"

"Fine. Come. Let's go."

Karen's father was wiry and had feral eyes. He bore the smell of living in his clothes. Karen introduced the actor. "This is my friend."

"Oh, the friend routine. He have a name?"

"No," Karen said.

"You have a name, friend?" Karen's father, whose own name was Bill, asked, ground his teeth, grinned.

"On occasion—but not tonight. Possibly tomorrow," the actor said.

"Fuck you. I know who you are, anyway. How'd you two meet?" Karen's father asked.

"At a rehab center," Karen said.

Karen's father laughed. Karen pulled a snide face. She knew she was acting in ways which were surprising, even alarming, the actor. But hell, when the occasion called—and it was calling—she could be bristly.

"So, who was the best piece you ever had?" Karen's father asked the actor. He had a tick when he spoke. Knots appeared around his mouth and jaw, then untied themselves. "Two categories," he went on. "Famous, first. Then nobodies."

"That's not a question I'm going to answer," the actor said.

Good for you! Karen thought.

"Hey, listen, your call," Bill said. "So—you want to make a bet?"

"You a casino?" the actor asked.

Yes! Karen thought.

"Ha ha! Rich as you are, I'll bet I'm carrying more money on me than you are."

"I'll pass," the actor said.

"So—not that I care, but—you fucking my daughter?"

"Watch your mouth," Karen said.

"You having sex with my daughter?" Bill grinned.

"No, I'm not," the actor said.

"A lot of actors are faggots—right?"

"Daddy—shut up, okay? Behave yourself." *Right conditions, right opportunity, and I could kill my father,* Karen thought. *Easily.*

Bill drew silent. Karen sensed the actor trying to take stage, redirect the conversation. But nothing formed. "I think you should do the comedy," Karen said.

Before the actor left, Karen told him that perhaps a day without dropping by might make sense. Then she and her father settled in. He produced over three hundred thousand from his duffle, which she put in a large stoneware pickling crock. He also plucked four bottles of Jameson scotch from his duffle, lined them up on her shelf. "When these are gone, *I* go," he said.

"Why don't you start now?" Karen suggested.

Her father grinned what he called his Irish grin, unscrewed a Jameson cap. "You have ice?" he asked.

"I do. Exactly where you'd expect," Karen said.

"Up your ass?"

"Fuck you," Karen said.

"Didn't you used to wait on me?" Bill grinned again.

"Well, here in Idaho, help's a bitch," Karen said.

The actor rapped on Karen's door at dawn. She had to step over her father, who lay spread across cushions and pillows. When she stepped into the screen, the actor held his palms up in apology. "I know, I know," he said, *sotto voce.* "I just wondered if you were okay, if you needed help."

"I don't know. Possibly. With what?"

The actor nodded toward the floor and her father.

"Well, maybe if you'd come to the door thirty-six years ago. But today, this morning, I think I've got it somewhere near control."

"Just thought I'd check."

"Have a good day," Karen said.

"Are you angry?"

"No, I'm—" *Angry? Do I get to choose?* "It's before six in the morning," Karen said.

"I know. I'm sorry." The actor lowered his head and turned away. Then turned back. "So, when you made the comment about *comedy* being the project I should do—were you serious?"

Karen's father worked his way through the first bottle and a half of Jameson the next day. He read two Ursula Le Guin books, slept a bit, drank, slid outside, watched his daughter throw pots on her wheel. "You two close?" he asked at one point. "You and the heartthrob?"

"We just met."

"I read—*People Magazine*, some place—about him and...I can't remember her name, some actress."

"Makes sense."

As if on cue, the actor slid by in his red Attak. Rolled. Waved. Karen waved back.

"You ever regret not staying with the nun thing?" her father asked.

If I had, at least it would have kept you off the compound, she thought. "You ask me that every time you drop by," she said.

"I wonder about it."

"Yeah, I can imagine," she said. "I'm sure."

"You'd've been good—a good nun. I believe that. Humble. Selfless. An empty vessel for your Savior. You'd've been a natural. So—can you throw enough of those every month to pay the bills?"

"I throw enough in a year to manage."

"You don't take shit from anybody, do you?"

"No, not if I can help it," Karen said.

The next morning, while her father moaned and tossed on the floor, Karen baked blackberry muffins. She brewed coffee, took half outside in a thermos, and left the rest on the stove. It was nice, setting her own routine. Being semi-in-charge, semi-dedicated. Mid-morning, the actor materialized. He waved. Her hands were on the mud of a pot. "Hi," she called.

"Hey, Fire Lady!" he called.

When he reached her, he stood and watched. "He still here?" he asked, finally. "The reprobate?"

"His plan is, he'll leave after the four bottles of Jameson are gone," Karen said. "He got through half yesterday. So who knows?"

"That's a lot of scotch."

"I wouldn't know. One good glass of Crown Royal, and I'm a slut. Well, not a slut exactly, but—"

There was a clatter inside, followed by what sounded like a body falling. Then Bill appeared, white-skinned and shirtless, framed by the screen. "So what's the plan?" he called out.

"There's muffins and coffee on the stove," Karen returned.

"You know, I've seen a bunch of your movies," Bill announced to the actor. "And I have to say—I don't get the excitement." Then he disappeared to assemble his breakfast.

"So, am *I* going to get to spend time with you today?" the actor asked.

"You really want to be a friend—you'll spend time with *him*. Keep him away from messing up my work schedule."

Just then, the door kicked open and Bill, carrying a plate of muffins and a mug, moved through—the screen clattering behind. He stepped off the porch and crossed to where Karen had set her wheel up on the redwood picnic table. He held out the plate of muffins.

"Thanks, but my hands are a bit preoccupied," Karen said.

"Muffin?" Bill asked, extending the plate to the actor.

"Is it all right?" the actor asked.

"They're community muffins," Karen said.

The actor took a muffin, and Karen's father took him by the elbow, hitched a nod toward the cabin. "Give the kiddo her peace," he said. "C'mon. I've got a treat for you inside."

The actor hesitated—a studied hesitation, then a shadowed smile. He checked Karen, whose eyes were straight ahead, where the smells of flint and muck spun centrifugally from her wheel's turning.

"Hey! Actor!" Bill prompted.

The two plodded onto the porch, then in. The door slapped. Karen took a huge breath. *Jesus, hallelujah!* she thought. Her bones felt lighter. The wind through the aspen seemed washed, liquid with hydrogen and the mixed songs of finch and jay. A family of teal drifted on the Payette. A blue heron took to the sky. Gravity seemed toying with a holiday.

And so she worked, at first expecting one of the two males to amble out, but neither did. So she stopped listening to her father's cabin-bound fits of coughing or growls of laughter—let anxiety go and simply worked.

She'd been focused nearly four hours when something like china shattering froze her. Then a spume of her father's obscenities. Then a lesser spume in the trained voice of the actor. Then body sounds. More body sounds. A cry of pain, immediately trailed by an animal vocalization of disbelief. Another cry. A thud. A silence. A peal of laughter—her father's. A second peal—the actor's.

The screen door kicked open and the two—her father still without a shirt, the actor with his tan tee, now torn—appeared, arms over each other's shoulders, each with a bottle of Jameson in his fist.

"He called me a reprobate!" the actor crowed.

"I like this son of a bitch!" Karen's father called.

"He thinks I should do either the CIA movie! Or the story of your life!" the actor bellowed.

They staggered forward. Karen could see blood seeping into the actor's shirt—blood discoloring and oozing from her father's pallid skin. Something lodged in her throat—a clot like raw, unfired clay. One monosyllabic question after another formed itself and rolled forward. None, though, found a voice.

"We taught each other a lesson!" her father crowed.

A proverb? A parable? Karen wondered.

"He thinks a mature, serious, political action film would nail down my acting reputation," the actor gloated. "He says I need to play someone soulless!"

"We sliced each other pretty well!" Karen's father set fingers to where whatever had done the slicing had opened his skin.

"We sliced each other pretty fucking well," the actor cawed—the obscenity punched with a stupid kind of self-consciousness. He lifted his shirt and displayed torn open flesh.

"To men!" Karen's father toasted. He tipped back the Jameson.

"To men!" the famous actor barked. And he did the same.

Right! To men and their absence! Karen was amazed—after her initial revulsion—at how calm she felt. The whole moment appeared as through an aerial camera.

"Whadaya think, kiddo? What's your evaluation? The old man's made a friend!"

"He has some amazingly good reasons," the actor said, "for the CIA film being my next project."

Karen stood. She walked over to her rain barrel, rinsed her hands. Behind her, the two men watched and giggled. She wiped her hands on the towel, entered the cabin, went to the pantry where she always hung her purse, plucked up a black Patagonia vest, and strode out. "I'll be back when I'm back," she said.

"Kiddo!" her father protested.

"Baby! Where're you going?" the actor slurred.

"*Baby?*" Bill chided.

Karen ground her keys into the ignition and peeled away.

Maybe it was time to move again. She was a browser of atlases. There was the north of Washington state; there was Oregon. Canada. There was Europe—Umbria in Italy; the north of Spain; Coimbra, Portugal. If she'd not given up the convent, days like today never would have happened. The aspen whizzed by. The lodgepole, the beaver ponds, the sage, Russian thistle. A family of sandhill crane convened in a meadow.

She was edging a hundred. The sky was blue, broken with double-ribbed white clouds—not a real sky, not a sky settled into any day or hour, month or season. A folk art sky. Karen gulped air from her open window.

For a couple hours, she left the highway and drove lumber roads. The ruts and washboards jostled her, made her ribs ache. The billowing dust made her choke. She yelled *Leave me alone!* out her window and startled a trio of elk, who bolted, made her slam on her brakes, kill the engine, and cry. Karen hated crying. It was so useless—how the tears shrank her face, how her lungs ached afterwards, how she raked through her hair with her fingers, always, when she broke down. She hadn't cried in a year. *Assholes! Bastards!*

She found her way back to the highway, drove at forty, took the turnoff, and climbed, over dirt again, to Stanley Lake, where she parked at the far end, got out, kicked off her sandals, and walked in until the water pooled over her head. She exhaled and let herself sink, closed her eyes, imagined herself afloat in a uterine animal membrane that would deliver her into a world ultimately kinder than the one she'd known.

When, finally, she kicked up and surfaced, the air was softer, the touch of day more careful and warm. It was okay. Would be. Things like this floated in, disrupted. Her father would leave; he always did. The actor would leave. He'd choose a project and believe it to be the project intended for him since the day he was born. He had that knack. Self-belief. He was a man with that capacity.

Karen sat on a fallen log. She let the sun and light ammonia fragrance of the water clear her mind—bring her back, dry her clothes, set her down, steady her. *And look! Look!* A moose moving into the lake a good hundred yards away. *Thank you, Somebody! Thank you!* She watched the huge, ungainly creature edge his muzzle into the water, saw his rack tip. She squinted to scramble the image, and the moose became an inverted root stump. *Good! Life at play! That is what life here in Idaho should be.*

An hour later, she stood, did a few stretches, slow and dancelike, then slipped into her sandals, moved lazily to the Outback. *Jesus, she had gotten it filthy!*

So, what were the boys up to now? Karen didn't even want to guess. They were becoming acquainted. They were being boys. And through it, the actor was undoubtedly getting Karen's father to parse *reprobate*, prescribe the next dozen years of his life.

It was possibly funny. Both men were approaching the same age. Yet the actor was a cartoon of a boy, and Bill a cartoon of a redneck. Son and father; father and son. If they'd been a law firm: *Reckless & Reckless.* Better still: *Reprobate & Reprobate.* Maybe they'd both be dead when she arrived.

It was past five. Karen wanted a drink, so she drove further into Stanley, to the Kasino Club. What sounded good? Did she need to be careful? Probably. "How about a Heineken?" she asked the bartender. Then, "I'm sorry, a Chardonnay. No, I was right the first time—a Heineken."

She sipped it—cold and right. There was a golf match on the bar television. She kept hearing the name—but where was he?—Tiger Woods. What month was it? What year? What day?

Returning to Lowman, Karen set the Outback's cruise control at fifty-five—something about discipline, something about moderation. She kept her windows down. Containment, discipline, moderation: all three seemed appropriate to the hour, the day, the shift of season. She needed stilling—not the full duskiness of Idaho rushing at her. About two miles from her cabin, she noted traces of smoke, a smell, as a one-time firefighter, she found herself vulnerable to.

She had developed a knack for tasting any fire's size: from

a nearby campsite's lone fire pit to a sprawling acreage out of control. This one, the char shadowing the air, was small, yet hardly innocent. This was not someone camping. Not even a half-dozen campsites readying for dinner. This was maybe a small meadow or a house—a step up from recreation and rife with carelessness, thick with accident.

And Karen was heading into it. Directly. Like some bird homing—or as if she were still working for the Park Service and taking a call. If she'd had one of those—*what? what were they called?*—Global Positioning Whatevers, she couldn't have been more on target.

It was, of course, her cabin. She could smell her clothes in the smoke, taste her furniture and few possessions. When she got within sight, there was the actor sitting by the fuming ruins, drinking a Guinness. He was shirtless, his tight skin sweating black. He was in a pose—hanging his head. *So this is Hollywood remorse*, Karen thought.

She pulled up. She got out. She stood.

"We tried," the actor said.

To do what? Karen thought. She crossed to the smoldering debris—the black and broken sketch of a stick house fuming before her.

"We don't even know how it started," the actor said.

How it started was: two assholes got drunk and were careless, Karen thought. She turned, looked at the actor. He was standing now, eyebrows raised, shaking his head. To his left, sitting on the table where she had left it, was her wheel. *Thank God, at least, for that!* And, beside the wheel, sat the fat, oversized pickle crock.

"He said look in this," the actor said, and gestured.

"He left?"

"He felt shitty."

"Yeah, I'm sure."

"We both did."

"Well—boys, I guess, will be boys," Karen said.

"There's money." The actor gestured again toward the crock.

"Did you settle your future?" Karen asked.

The actor hesitated, briefly. "I'm going to do the CIA project," he said.

"Where you play a reprobate."

"But sympathetic."

"But sympathetic. Right. Good."

"You think so?"

"Absolutely. Only choice—no question. Now, please—leave. Do whatever. Drift your kayak. Leave me alone."

"Check the—"

"Don't worry! I will! I heard. Please leave."

"We tried to put it out."

"Yeah, well—fire's willful."

"I never thought that. That's well said. That's true."

"Please…" Karen held her palms out in front of her, shoulder high, as if she were going to push something—something very large, very resistant. "Okay?"

"Okay," the actor said. He gathered his shirt, shook his head, shuffled away, across the mulch of pine and onto the path that led the half-mile to his cabin.

Karen moved to the burn again and stared in. She'd done her lingering when investigators rummaged fires for signs of negligence or arson. Flash points. She fought an urge to lift one of the raw timbers with her bare hand, feel its exhausted balsa weight. Maybe if, with concentration like prayer, she focused, then her hand wouldn't blister. Perhaps she could purify herself against second- or third-degree burns. *Why not!* She had spent entire years renouncing her flesh, mortifying the sad, skin-sack envelope of herself. *Hey, give it a try. Show the world of flames who's boss.* She reached, knew the skin of her hand would only bubble and pop. She wasn't ready for whatever grace or miracle, not today.

She kicked at embers, shards. A cloud—half smoke, half

ash—rose up and stung her eyes, made her gag briefly.

She turned and wandered to where her wheel stood on the picnic table, touched it, ran her hand over its rim. *Circle*, she thought. *Axis*. Finally, her eyes slipped to the pickling crock near the wheel, the one thing her father and the actor had saved. She reached toward its lid, which still radiated heat, so she bunched her shirt in her hand, gripped the lid-knob, lifted, and set it aside. Within, she could see, there was a note. A note and what appeared to be all the loose currency her father had arrived with. She withdrew the note. It read: *Onward & Upward*, and was scrawled with something she assumed to be her father's version of a signature.

Karen wandered to the river, crouched. Every river was different, every river she'd known. The Payette was a singer. If you listened, you could hear its several voices—notes humming from where a rock broke the current here, a log there. It was a song you could listen to for a long time. Karen dropped her hands in the drift, let them add their own notes, let them be quieted and lulled. They needed song; they needed cleaning; they needed to lose any accusation or judgment that might clench them.

Maybe, one by one, the digits of her hands would leave her and float away, become—she laughed—fingerlings, independent as alewife, lithe and long as river grass.

ANGEL OF DEATH

I started the First Church of Idaho because of Love.

My veterinary father was a godless man by choice—not a sinner, more a heathen: a man legion with restlessness and impatience, a person leeched of Love. If you drew close, he'd look away. If you came near, he would lift a tool or newspaper, power the television, stand up, clear the table, go off, remember a blood test he had to check, take a bath. If you entered a room, he would leave. There was no passion in him, no ecstasy, no moment of sacrament—all of which left a hole, an emptiness, a yearning.

I was born in Alton, New Hampshire, and though the Anabaptists came, erected tents, no measurable God accompanied them. I know; I looked. I walked their grounds, lifted tent flaps, looked in, heard their voices coiling up like smoke, listened. God is Love and Love, God. But, for me, no Love, no God of blood or ejaculation made circuit or arrived in that small town beside the wide lake—a lake so vast a god could easily have risen from it, Love-drenched in mist.

And there was no God, no Love, in Barnstable, Massachusetts—not in the gabled house or in my tense father's cinder-block shelter-clinic. None in Mille Lacs, Minnesota. And I wondered: was it the wind? The ice? If God was breath, if the Love he brought was all air and sky—could He freeze? And was all that snow in Mille Lacs parts of Him flaking off? Falling, failing, filling the winter with who He was? But then—wouldn't He be used up?

But no; God was infinite—wasn't that the Truth? Reverend Cowper had said that. And He'd so sacrificed Himself, or part thereof, every winter, that he might fill up Minnesota. It seemed possible. It seemed beautiful, even.

I was doing my plane geometry at a table among swabs and alcohol. I took the lid off the alcohol, sniffed to see whether I could smell God—because the smell, sort of, was like air at minus twenty outside. "Have you ever smelled God? And does he smell cold?" I asked my father.

"Do your homework," my father said.

I asked, "So—is there an *animal* God, do you think? A Divine Veterinarian?"

And my father, hands washing down something, said, "What are you talking about?"

"God, the Father," I said. "God who delivers Love and carries Life and Death in his two hands."

"I know Abyssinian cats," my father said. "I know Wheaton terriers. I know logarithmic goats." And he laughed.

"I've been looking for God," I told my near-angel mother.

"Tell me if you find him," my mother said.

"I think *you* could bring God into this house," I said. "I do." I was fourteen; we were on the outskirts of Tulsa—in a ranch house beside a ranch house serving as another clinic.

"Oh, sweetie," she said. "Sweetie. Yes, I know, I could. I might. I might bring God into the proper house—but not to a man who can't settle."

"Is it because Great-Grandfather owned a railroad?" I asked.

"Baby, the Devil is always money that isn't yours," my mother said. "Watch the horses. See, always, how the horses shy from your father's touch."

Sometimes I slept with my mother. "Feet on the pillow, close to my head," she would say, and I would descend to sleep, she holding my ankles, kissing the soles of my feet. "It's all right this way," she'd say. It was on nights my father slept next door at the clinic. "I wanted to talk," my mother would tell me. "He said, *Not now*. He said, *What I'm thinking about now is Austin, Texas*." She called my father's restlessness a raven. She said it was a dark bird. "He's a good man," she'd say. "But his moving here—here, there—is evil."

Put a cross on any building, I will enter it. Something in me—secret, deep—my family's moving, my mother's sleeping hands on my feet, a song I heard once—*Message of the Cross.*

If there is a secret under another person's skin, I want it. If there is a mystery inside another's flesh, mortified, every nerve in me is desire. And that's the Cross. Which, of course, is Love. Something intercepts something. Something touches—lips to labia; labia, lips—something enters, goes through, something crosses.

Tell me every time you fell in love, a woman said to me once. And I told stories from the first grade, third grade, sixth grade—each containing more crossing, more intersecting, than the last, each hoping for more, something new, and each bearing larger and more undoing disappointments.

First, with six-year-old Connie, it was only hair—the way it fell. The light hit it, shone through, and it smelled unlike mine, not of soap, more like the wings of birds, or pine needles.

I told stories of held breath, electricity, appearance and disappearance—like magic, approaching and never arriving, never arriving until it did, or almost did—almost—with the woman who said, *Tell me every time you fell in love*. Not arriving, finally, even then, feeling the pain then deeper pain of distance; until...and then until...and until.

You ask: *What is the First Church of Idaho*? I say: *In the beginning*...and mention my mother's hands, my ankles, my father's corrupting restlessness. I say I enter any building under a cross. I remember *tell me every time*. I use the word *intersection*.

Blood will enter this story: bones, fire, poison. This is, after all, a religious story, charred and of blood conversion, liturgy with a flamed razor. I don't mind speaking in tongues; I embrace it. The woman I love speaks in tongues—then not. She moves in and out, at once serpent and hostess—often confusing the two. She is twice blessed: blessed by God, blessed by the oyster bed.

What am I saying? What am I talking about? It doesn't matter, just listen. I am speaking in tongues. Because it is, of course, the tongue that connects us, that redeems us, that sets us free. *I often think, these days, of oral sex*, the woman I love says. *Both ways.* And there are my own flames that occur, reading her words. And the sense that the burning which has been promised will fail to happen. But I've been wrong before.

And before that—wrong.

But, these things said, best we move on to Idaho. Which is where I came nearly a year and a half ago. As an adult. As a Believer. As someone hungry in more and more desperate ways to ascend through Love. Through God. Or is it *de*scend. As the woman I love says, *Whichever.*

There are Angel of Death mushrooms in Idaho. They grow in the high meadows around sage. Their stems taper; their gills, like flesh, are pink. Careless reapers sometimes mistake Angel of Death for vision mushrooms—both take your breath—but the Angel of Death are merciless. They paralyze in a minute; seeking medical attention is unthinkable. Heart and brain uncouple, forget each other in a millisecond. The First Church of Idaho is precisely seven miles from marshy flats strewn with Angel of Death.

When I was fifteen, I sang in a choir. I loved the organ. I loved the chancel as well; the sacred tendons in my neck strained in song. I sang with women my age, and I looked among them. Might one be there to love? But there was only Elizabeth Harrison who, even at fifteen, I knew, was filled with shame, and shame wasn't my passion. Besides, Elizabeth Harrison's hair smelled too much like milk.

The same year I sang, I had a vision. One day, I believed, I would lead a congregation. I heard our new reverend introduced by his beautiful wife—*This is Reverend Cowper. He leads*—and the phrase stuck: *He leads*. Someday, I would have a beautiful woman standing beside me, saying, *This is...He leads. This is...*

Except—on an April day after school, I went to sit alone in the chancel, hear myself and the choir in my head, and pray. The church was locked. The Parish House as well. I thought, *If church is yet another place locked to the yearning heart, I will not have it.* So I set dreams of leading a congregation aside.

I left home when I was eighteen. Went to college, left college, went to another, and another. I studied philosophy, poetry, religion. I studied marine biology, astronomy. I traveled north into Alaska, where I hoped I might live with the Inuit, but hope is folly. I traveled south on a bicycle, camped among basalt boulders and in the shadows of Navajo sandstone. I fell under the spells of nearly breathtaking women—one who dried flowers and sold them to shops, another who repaired bicycles and figured scrimshaw.

I talked to Buddhists, Seventh-day Adventists, Mormon elders. I went to graduate school, left, wondered why I'd gone. For a year, I composed music—for myself only—gave all the music sheets away one night to another person my age I met, camping, in Escalante, Utah. Then I began to hear my songs, most of them, a year later, on the radio.

What is it about music?

What is it about the woman I love? And the Angel of Death mushroom?

Did I mention the fire and my mother's death? I've been in a hurry here. I'm sorry. She ran toward me, barefoot, down a hall, burning, a saint in flame. I'd come home to, then, North Dakota. Because certain North Dakota birds and North Dakota cattle interested my father. He'd stayed at the clinic that night. And was—he had a word—*filtrating*. What is filtrating? And my mother—maybe it was a toaster, a hairdryer, something wrong in its wiring—but a fire had broken out. And I was asleep. Dreaming of God. Someday, a church, a cross. A woman to save me. Love that was *Love*. An intersection.

But dreams have their way. Or will. And I woke to choking. Smelled incineration and hadn't the presence to touch my doorknob, measure, decide. So I turned it. And there was my mother—angel that she was. All light! All ball of flame! Her nightgown. Midstride. The world freezes itself, even in fire, gives us photographs.

Then the ceiling collapsed. And she, angel, was no more. The house ceased being a house; she ceased being my mother. It's what can happen when the world opens full stop and in the presence of God. "Mother!" I screamed. But to no worldly purpose. Because I learned, that night, what ejaculation was. To dust. To ashes.

I sold everything; it meant nothing. I robbed a liquor store. I thought: *I will do something right and something wrong—and, out of that, a thing perfectly true will be opened.* I traveled to Italy, Genoa. In the fifth grade, my school did a play about Columbus. I was ten. I played an old sailor talking to Columbus. I chewed a corncob pipe—Johnson's baby powder, which I could puff to look like ancient smoke, in its bowl. The play pretended a pier in Genoa.

How long before the sacrifice of my father did I meet the woman I love? Two and a half years? It was far from Idaho and on an island—where I had come to do just that: be on an island. Wake to egret and pelican, to sand so white that, when tread on, it made the submerged sound of scallop and oyster—valve, mollusk, distant aching.

I was on a wide porch; the sky flat and metallic with all the promise of night. I held a glass—vodka, ice. There was music.

Hello, a voice, lovely, said. *Hello. I'm the person you're supposed to meet.* And I smiled. As I will smile, always, when transgression pretends at innocence. *Hello*. Simple enough. Not a moment, certainly, turning itself from softest sea marsh to the corruption of corruption—miles away, years away—in the serrated cradle of mountains, in the shadow of a cross.

What followed occurred with an inevitability and logic bearing no sense beyond whatever the raw truth is of oyster beds, mimosa, dolphin, the voice of a once-gospel singer, the squall of a cat. Tongues. Talk in tongues. We were two people who had trusted in He-thought-to-be-God—only to be denied. We were two people shown the violence asleep in Desire. We were two people who learned that Faith can blind people.

You're not following this. It's all right. The point is Love. The point is God. The point is there we were.

She, the woman I was supposed to meet, placed filaments of island—sand, shell, grass—in envelopes, after I'd left. Mailed them. I sent her the smooth stones of riverbeds. She sent sharks' teeth, ibis feathers. I sent salmon eyes, pinion bark, turquoise. We met on balconies all over North America, always, though, with the unspoken hope of Idaho. The grace and the light of a riverwater that, in Idaho only, might be God.

Then, when all seemed perfect—a cherished life, myself together with the woman I was supposed to meet—my father wrote: *You can't hide!* Impatient—he'd done some tracking. He kept fox feet, puma and coyote paws, in formaldehyde, and studied them. *You probably thought Idaho a safe notion*, his letter began. *But veterinary medicine makes men crafty. The First Church of Idaho?* he wrote. *I'll believe it when see it.* Threat and necessity seeped from his words.

"It will be fine. Allow him. Reconcile," the woman I love, Lyla, said. She was with me then. "Don't suffer the past. You survived, I survived mine. Forgive. Be kind." I thought, *Of course, certainly, forgive, allow,* and felt strangely clean and generous.

Except!

Except I failed to take account, when she spoke, of a shape—half-man, half-dog—black and immense, behind her. Lyla, I knew, knew pain, had lived damage. What I did not know was of her life still stalked by Evil.

On a Wednesday, my father arrived. He had driven a Mercury Cougar over Galena Summit and looked diminished in it. "I've been hybridizing Arabians and Appaloosa, south of Hailey," he said as he stepped out. "For a week." He wore black jeans, a leather vest. An unopened San Miguel sweated in his fist.

"Jesus—you can't leave it alone," I said.

"San Miguel?" my father said. "Or veterinary medicine?" He laughed. "So, First Church of Idaho! Bring it on! Give me your best sermon." Did he look taller? Shorter?

"If you could make any creature not itself, you would," I said.

"Oh, Charlie—Charlie, Jesus!" my father said.

"What?"

"Maybe I practice on animals to be ready," he said.

"For?"

"Shit, anything. You. The Nobel Prize. Myself. Being seventy-two."

I looked over at a row of cabins at the river's edge—every one unowned, every one a satellite.

He went on. "I serve the best of blood and bone and brain." Was his voice proud? Terrified? "Am I not allowed?" he boomed on. "I thought this was America. A melting pot. Am I wrong? Do you have evidence to the contrary? Welcome home," my father said.

"Right, welcome home," I said. Then thought, *Home? What is he talking about?*

"Obviously, you blame me for the death of your mother—right?" my father said.

I looked away. I barked like a dog—a schnauzer. I barked a second time. Anything in me that wished to be merciful grew infected. The woman I love came up and stood beside me.

"Lyla," she announced to my father, and held her hand out.

He looked wary. "Well—you had to be someone," he said.

"And it's true. I am." She smiled.

"Good for you," my father said. "Most of us aren't." He took her hand.

"This is very different from where I've been," Lyla said. "Here. Idaho. The—what do they get called? The Sawtooths. I've been in the Caribbean mostly."

"Right, no bandicoot here," my father said. "No sand turtle. Though I saw an alpaca."

"It was a llama," the woman I love said. They seemed a match for each other.

"Alpaca," my father said. "Sorry. I beg to differ."

"Always the begging to differ," I said, explaining my father. "Can't help himself."

"Charlie, have you become a pain in the ass? As a man of God? We all beg," my father said. "In business, they call it solicitation. But beg for *some*thing." And he smiled, nodded his head, looked strangely precarious and lonely. "Lyla," he said.

"Yes," she said. "Cherokee. Cherokee by way of Le Havre. My great-grandfather was an Inca."

"Been around," my father said.

"Yes—and *around*," the woman I love said.

"Show me your church," my father said.

I laughed. "Right. Show me *yours*," I said.

"I need to see this church, my son's church. The First Church of Idaho," he said. And laughed.

"Not until you're baptized," I said. And Lyla looked, suddenly, alarmed.

My father walked away. Stood, back to us. There were strands of foam floating on the river. My father crouched, scooped one out, smeared his forehead, stood, turned back. "Baptized—bap-*tized*!" he said. And he laughed—a boom of recklessness and, almost, fear. "Certainly would be a first," he said.

"I suspect, finally, that's the point," I said.

"Do you have an altar?" he said. He tabbed open his beer. "Pews? An apse? A pain in the apse? Stained glass? Do people kneel at the sound of your voice? Do you have an organ?"

"I tell you what, why not go back—hybridize some more horses?" I said.

"Charlie. You always remarked to your mother that I lacked time. For you—*wah wah wah*, lacked time. Except—*voila*, here I am! Time made! All yours! And you seem scarcely—why don't you seize the moment, reveal yourself! Show me what you're about!"

"So you agree?" I said. "To being baptized."

"Baby—" Lyla touched my shoulder.

"I thought you were making a joke," my father said.

"Careful," Lyla cautioned.

"Joke?"

"Baby, don't. He's come for—"

"Joke? No. No, when you came over Galena, you left comic Idaho. This is *ecstatic* Idaho. This is the inspirational. This is where your breath becomes a gift. Or is taken away."

"And this baptism—?"

"Baby?" Lyla had the sense of a thing inside me run wild.

"It's at the edge of a pond," I said. "In a meadow. Fifteen miles."

"So you're serious."

Lyla moved behind, pressed as close as another human might, encircled me.

"You seem to have fallen into some good fortune," my father said. He smiled at Lyla. "I confess to being surprised."

"Well, the breathtaking will do that," I said. "Surprise." *What was this fury, exactly? Why was I so enraged?*

My father shifted, face hardening. He gazed over the Salmon River, across a hillside of grazing Angus, at the Sawtooths. The sound of the river rolled like a thousand stones. Steelhead held perfectly still, tails flat against boulders, in the current. It was a moment of waiting, and I was happy to have and enter it. I thought: *If the hall of our burning house had been this river! If my angel mother had run toward me on it!*

Lyla's eyes eddied, brewed murky. "What are you seeing?" I whispered.

"A black dog," Lyla whispered back.

My father laughed; he shook his head. "Baptism," he said. He looked abandoned. Sad.

"Call it what you will," I said.

"Oh, really? What *I* will?" my father said.

"Sure. Why not."

"I'll call it superstition, then," my father said. "I'll call it folly. But, really, who am I? I'm an atheist seeking grace."

"So, if it doesn't bring you to your knees—it's both?" I quizzed. "Folly? Grace?"

"Baby. You aren't thinking—" Lyla began.

"So—what do you say, my car or yours?" my father said.

"Yours is a rental, right?" I said.

"Is! Absolutely is. Hertz number one!" my father said.

"We'll take mine," I said. I looked at Lyla. "We'll take ours."

The highway, Idaho 57, rises and falls, gelled by heat phantoms. Always at night—elk. During the day—cattle, horses. Red-tails and harriers ride the thermals. You'll see heartleaf and larkspur—thick as taste, soft as a coverlet—stretching here, billowing there—on either side of the road. There's the cutoff to Stanley Lake, a thatch of mining roads. You can get lost everywhere.

You can get lost in your heart, especially. Afternoons, before Lyla finally said, *Yes, I'll come*, I would gas my Cherokee and set out. Everything, dirt roads. Ruts. Abandoned camps. *Please come and be in this*, I thought. Because I had written, proposed. And she would write or call back. *I'm supposed to be there*, she'd said. *I know that. I believe that. But...not yet, this isn't quite the time.*

The three of us headed out in the Cherokee—Lyla and I in front, my father in back. I had a single, caramel-colored plastic Foodtown bag I'd brought.

"Funny, I've always been taught that the men sit up front," my father said.

"Who taught you that?" I asked.

"It was a joke," my father said.

"I don't think so," I said.

"You never understood my humor—that was our problem," my father said.

"Name one person who did," I said. "One."

"I had a malamute once," my father said. "And *he* laughed."

The wheels rolled. The macadam rippled. The sun dropped—five degrees, ten—in the northwest. "There was a massive fire up here two summers ago," I said. "Charred everything."

"So—I'm smelling something. I guess that's what I'm smelling." my father said.

"I don't understand what you're—"

"The smoke," he said. "Even with the windows rolled up, I smell smoke."

"What you smell—" Lyla turned so that he might understand. "Is what the smoke *became*."

"Being?"

"The everlasting *danger* of smoke," Lyla said. "Smoke pretending to be dusk. Smoke pretending to be shadow."

"So—are you a mystery writer?" my father asked.

"God's a mystery writer," I injected.

"Straight from the mouth of the pastor of the First Church of Idaho," my father mocked.

We turned north on Sand Mountain Road. Where it had been washed out, we swung the Cherokee wide through gilia and blue flax. There were stretches of barbed wire staked with metal but no visible cattle. Redwings stared cautiously but held their ground. Someone had recently doused a campfire, stacked it over with rocks. Vapor—half steam, half ash—slid out and up from between the boulders.

"I can't get a handle on whether this is good country or bad country for a veterinarian," my father said.

"I'm told veterinarians stay," I said.

"That doesn't feel like an answer to my question."

"I didn't think you'd asked a question."

"Jesus, for such a watchful child, you've gotten almost combative," my father said.

"The truth," I said.

"Oh, yes, I'm sure, of course—the truth. At the age of forty-four! You're the pastor. Hallelujah," my father said.

We drove perhaps a half mile in silence. Lyla took my hand; she traced the inflated veins with a nail. I thought of the same nail, which, in our passion, had more than once drawn blood. Thin air from the slightly open passenger window riffled the Foodtown bag.

"So, how do you know—when this road forks—left or right?" my father asked.

"I've been here. I've traveled it," I said.

"But if you're a first-*time* traveler."

"The main road, Sand Mountain—if you look carefully, you can see—is just a bit wider, gets more traffic."

"Possibly. But I've looked. And I can't see any difference."

"And I can't help you beyond what I've said."

From the crest of a rise—earlier road mud, scabbed and flaked on either side—an enormous meadow, then pond, stretched long and wide to our left. Croppings of rock too—all riddled. I slowed, hovered almost. Sometimes a pause absorbs pleasure; sometimes it identifies a doubt, a question. My slowing, my hovering, seemed both. Who was the man behind me? Why was he here? And the light wasn't the light we'd approached in. It was a new light—one, it seemed, bearing purpose, a patient light, which had been waiting and understood, fully, why it was there.

"So is this where someone calls out, 'This is the place'?" my father said.

Neither Lyla nor I responded. I shifted the Cherokee down, engaged, and the pause we were in stopped.

"Well, it *is* beautiful country—I'll give it that," my father said. "No railroad here? No trains?"

Neither Lyla nor I responded.

"Looks like it could be colder than hell, though," my father said. "In the winter."

"Winter's severe—true, you're right," I said.

We snaked down, avoiding washouts, eluding ruts.

"This land is everything I dreamed," Lyla said.

There was a sense of my father's heightened vigilance in the Cherokee when we pulled over. I opened my door; Lyla opened hers. I took up the Foodtown bag. We got out. My father sat, face against a back window, and—cut off as he was—he looked cut from paper—worn, yellowed, flat—like a bad photograph of himself. He had the eyes of a person looking from the tight, protected inside of a car at torrential rain.

"What you're thinking of doing, you don't need to do," Lyla said.

"Rites of passage," I said.

"What you're thinking of doing, you don't need to do," Lyla repeated.

The back handle of the Cherokee door cracked. And the washed photo of my father in its hard frame gave way to his moving from where he'd ridden, slipping out, setting his feet on the pregnable ground. "Isn't there some sort of Baptist song about the river?" my father asked.

"I'm sure," I said.

"There are many," Lyla said.

"So is this total immersion or partial?" my father asked. He grinned. "Just curious. And are you going to read something from your own book—or from the Bible?"

"My own book?"

"Hey, it's your church. People write. It's possible," he said. "And it would have pleased your mother. She adored writers. I tried writing once."

Lyla's hand was in mine. "Why don't we walk?" she said.

So we did—my father launching a monologue; myself, stooping to pick mushrooms, usually beside broad clusters of ripe sage. Each time I spotted and crouched, I could feel pressure, restraint, feel Lyla pull. I could feel the tractable, long tendons of her arms hold me back. Still, by the time we reached the edge of the pond, I had a full two dozen Angel stems and caps.

I mention my father's monologue. His almost-in-tongues oration. It was unlike him—a meander, a prattle, a ramble. He spoke of Canadian geese and ocelot, boa constrictors and a runt hamster. He went on about a three-legged goat. He kept using words like *determination* and *gene pool.* There was an erratic story about a young mandrill separated from its parents, then sold out of a pet store in Atlanta to a landfill engineer who moved to Tulsa then to Solvang, California. "The man called me," my father said, "and said, 'I have a crying mandrill. Ever seen a crying mandrill? Do you know if mandrills cry? Is it characteristic? Because, you know—I love this crazy monkey. I love him. But he cries. All the time. And if there's a thing—especially something simple—I can do—something, because I don't know monkeys—then I will do it. Tell me what you think.'"

My restless veterinarian father talked of birds after the mandrill story. Livestock. He talked of ferret and mink. Skunk. Raccoon. Pelican. Grebe. It was as if something had been released, set loose. This after a life of smugness, of distance and disdain. I thought: *I do not know this man—never saw him—but he is a man I could love.* Yes, of course, because we were in Idaho, after all. Lyla was moving, moving like spring water beside me. And there was all the power of the First Church.

I don't know why I did what I did next, said what I said. Perhaps it was the place, the Life and Death of it—the Love. Everything was the power I'd sought always. The light of God. The beauty and tragedy of crossing. Nothing was absent. "Remove your shoes," I instructed.

My father paused, complied. Something played across his face—rue, maybe, or knowing.

In the gelatin air, dragonflies. Lyla watched, scanned, read my father to the bone. When he was barefoot—his brow humble, nearly—he indicated his shoes, marked his compliance.

I slipped a hand into the mushrooms. I drew my hand out. "Your pants, your vest, your shirt, everything," I said.

Again, my father paused—no deflecting words, no impatient posturing or mockery. A kestrel swooped into the meadowed basin, rose with a small snake. The light where we all stood took discrete shape, a body—living and creaturely. Then, over the shoulder, so to speak, of the body and its reverberant light, I could see a shadow, which—given the blank, cloudless sky—was impossible; still, a man, head all but contorted on his neck. And a black dog.

"Jesus God, no!" Lyla said—her voice smothered. But my father heard her, sensed something, checked the air. Then he began to slip items above his head, off his shoulders, down from his hips. He stepped out and out of them. And when he did, the shadow, which had done all but speak, disappeared, leaving only its pulsing and carnal after-shade.

Lyla leaned in, said, "We need to go back."

"No," I said.

"Please," she said.

"So the anointed whisper," my father said. He seemed oddly shamed, penitent.

I reached into the mushrooms.

"Your hands shake," my father said.

I drew an Angel of Death out—the draw more a question than intent.

"What he sees is right," Lyla advised. "Your hands—"

I broke the cap, extended it. "Hold that," I told my father.

I could feel pain surge in Lyla, flood. We were—Lyla and I both knew—only brief tenants in a ravening world which could be fully jubilant, merciful, but cruelly vengeful.

But wait! Was there a voice? I heard something in the wide, carnal and gutted air—a breath, a shadow—speak privately to Lyla. *Come, Daughter*, it urged. *Come. Why not? Do this! The flesh strangling itself is interesting! Go along! Pretend! You've been given the power! We all wear masks all the time! Don't be a child! You gave childhood up! Enjoy your knowledge!* It was a voice wishing to devour an entire landscape.

And Lyla stood—face overwhelmed with sorrow, with shame, with tears. It was a place—even in the not-knowing of it—that I had hoped to save her from since I'd first known her.

A second time, she leaned in. "This is why it took me so long," she said. "To choose Idaho, to come here."

I stroked her hair, kissed her eyes, reached in, took another mushroom, broke its cap. My father stood. Ready. Waiting. *The hardest thing about creation*, I thought, *is destruction*. The need each has for the other.

Lyla was shaking. My father waited, watching us. "We get old," he said. "We drown in shame." I broke a third cap for myself and moved to set it on my tongue, so that I might feel the bane of it alive and, in its way, all-powerful.

Lyla, neck like a swan, stretched up and kissed me full, brutal, on the mouth—would not let the kiss go, would not let the kiss go, then did. She regarded me. I began to undress. Lyla followed. I pressed the cap into my palm, and it felt like the head of a baby. Then, naked—like my father and like the woman I will always love—knew, believed, held the Angel of Death. Was this why my father had come? This, now, what he had hoped for, anticipated?

"Has she done this before? Have you done this before?" he asked Lyla.

Lyla could barely breath.

"You don't have to say—" I began.

"I've done everything before," Lyla said. "That's the problem. In my mind. Think of a thing done to another, I can recite it. You have another question?"

"Not right now, I think," my father said.

"Just as well, probably," Lyla said. She turned, looked at me, knew she had gone beyond the shadow of the man and the dog and was ready to bleed out her life with mercy or die. "Baby?" she said. "Are we doing this?"

"Too late now," I said.

"Too late now," Lyla reported to my father, and, with that, gazed west, where the late light, thickened by hatch, was entirely marbled and the color of roe.

"Too late now," my father laughed. "Too late now. What I've been thinking for years," he said.

And so, Death in our hands and in a blood world pocked with dots like eggs, we three—father, son, and the woman adored—set our toes into the water, mud squeezing between them like a mother's fingers. And we began walking into the water. Because it was, finally, Idaho. Because it was—all said and done, nothing left to say—the First Church.

THE CONSERVATIONIST & THE STORYTELLER

The conservationist had two families—first marriage, second marriage—and this confused him. Or perhaps *crowded* is a better word. Blake Fisher was a man of generous affections, but when his family circle increased, his stress rose. And when that happened, he often fled.

Where Blake fled was a ranch in Tetonia, Idaho, whose stream and ponds and grasslands he'd restored. Escaped, he'd read. He'd fish. He'd write what he called *monographs*—gathered memories, searching reflections—attempts to name the life-tributaries of his own river: industrialist, banker, university dean. Sometimes he'd meet a local ecologist—stream-biologist, ornithologist—for coffee. Evenings, he'd drive State Highway 33 into Driggs or Victor, sit by himself in a place like the Royal Wolf or Knotty Pine. He'd have a medium-rare steak and fries—ice cream for dessert—and listen to a group like the Hot Buttered Rum String Band.

This early October night, he was heading to the Knotty Pine when he spotted a blue Ford Focus pulled over in the gravel of East 3500 South, which connected his ranch to Idaho 33. The car's service lights were blinking.

Blake slowed. Perhaps a hundred yards away, he could see someone in the Focus. Then, that the someone was a woman. Finally, that it was a woman with a large hat. He pulled even and rolled down his window. The woman's window was open. She was perhaps ten years younger than he was— Blake guessed early sixties.

"You okay?" he asked.

"Fine—but I think the car's not," the woman said. She had

a smile that would rip rain out of a clear sky, make any storm ashamed.

"Out of gas?"

"Power, more likely." The woman in the hat smiled again, a smile that, if it were battery trouble, would start the car. "Out of power."

"I'll pull over—have a look," Blake said. And when he did—looking under the hood, having her turn the key, fiddling with wires—it seemed to him that, whatever the problem, it was (1) electrical, and (2) complicated.

Now the woman was out and standing by him. "I know nothing about car engines," she said. "But—right?—this shouldn't happen. It's a rental. Enterprise. Salt Lake."

"True, it shouldn't happen," Blake said. "But does. Like a lot of my life: shouldn't've happened, but did. You, at least, get to send the bill to Enterprise."

The woman laughed. Some spunkiness in her laugh made Blake laugh, then pause, then laugh again. And though he loved that he was laughing, he hadn't the least notion what he was laughing at.

"I'm Betsy," the woman introduced. "Betsy Barker. Actually Betsy Barker Smith, but the Smith is silent. As in Smith's Food King. So I'm Betsy Barker. That's my stage name."

They shook hands. "Blake," Blake said. "Blake Fisher. I have a spread, well, *place* not far away, just down the road."

Betsy Barker told Blake she'd been in a festival—"Storytelling. I'm a storyteller,"—on the other side of the Tetons, Jackson Hole. "Jackson Hole's like a bad painting of the West, I suspect," she said. "I told three different nights. The festival ended and I thought I'd drive over to the other side of the Tetons. Most of my life's been devoted to checking out the other side."

Again, Blake laughed. This time he had a better sense of why. *Why*, he felt sure, had mostly to do with his having spent the greater part of his life, as well, checking out the other side.

Blake suggested they abandon the Focus—"Well, I don't mean *abandon*, but..."—and that Betsy join him at the Royal Wolf for dinner. Then, if she didn't think he was being too forward, she could be his guest at the ranch that night. "It's not the Four Seasons. But it's, I like to think, generous. We have rooms for two or three families. And locks. On the doors. I tend to hide out, keep to myself, anyway. It'll be much quieter than a hotel. And then, tomorrow, I have some good, local mechanic friends who, I suspect, can get your Focus back into A-1 order. What do you say?" Blake finished.

"I say, *my goodness*!"

"So is that my goodness yes or no?"

"I think just a big *my goodness*!"

Blake drove to the Royal Wolf, where they shared a bottle of Red Diamond Cabernet—Betsy Barker with a trout dinner and Blake with a steak. "Should I remove my hat?" Betsy asked, soon after they'd been seated.

"Up to you," Blake said.

She hung it on a coat peg. "Hats are my weakness," Betsy said. "And I'm going to leave it at that. And now!" Betsy Barker smiled. "And now! The lady compromising herself is going to ask the gentleman compromising her to tell her about his life." She laughed.

Blake laughed and—was it the Red Diamond and the hour?—launched into stories he had only scribbled in longhand on stacks of yellow, thin-lined legal pads. About his Mormon boyhood in Idaho. About his crazy, philanthropic uncle in Fillmore, Utah. About his service in the Navy. His Mormon wife. His anti-Mormon wife. His accumulated seven children. "If I've done anything right in this crazy world, it's possibly being a good father," he said. And his voice caught. His eyes clouded.

When her host's voice caught and eyes clouded, Betsy Barker stretched an arm and put a hand over his laborer's hand and said, "I can see you're a good man. Already, tonight, you have *been* a good man. Several times. And oh, dear, yes: children. Later I will tell you about mine. Stories. Because, after all, I'm a storyteller. But yes…yes, my new good friend, Blake—Blake Fisher—children."

A band began setting up, testing amps, fiddling with a lightboard, climbing ladders, inserting colored gels in overhead spots. The drum set said THE BUFFALO BURGERS.

"Locals," Blake said, nodding to the band. "How's your trout?"

"My trout's good. How's your steak?" Betsy asked.

"My steak's good. And perfectly done. They do a nice job here," Blake said.

They left The Buffalo Burgers to the younger crowd and drove back to Blake's ranch in silent contemplation. When they reached her Focus, Betsy asked Blake to pull over. "I've a small bag," she said, and retrieved it. When they drew away, she waved a finger at the idle Ford. "Behave yourself," she said.

Back at the ranch, Blake secured Betsy in a far room and built a fire. He intended to read or write, but she appeared in a quilted housecoat and asked if she might trouble him for more wine. "I'm a sot," she said. Then added, "That's a joke."

He searched his fridge, checked an antique breakfront, then spotted a bottle of red sitting on a sideboard. "I'm not a kitchen person," he confessed. "I'm not a meal person, truth told. I've always depended on my wives—although I'll take anybody with domestic skills. Or the restaurant. But I'm sure there's an opener somewhere around here. A drawer. Somewhere. If we can find it, do you know how to—?"

"I do."

They found it, and Betsy opened the bottle, poured them each a glass. They sat on either side of the fire.

"Is this a compromising situation?" Betsy asked. "For you? Does it feel as such? A moonlit night, a strange woman in eveningwear? Sharing wine around a fire?"

"Oh…" Blake reddened.

"I'm sorry. I didn't mean to—"

"How about yourself? You're married—yes? This seem compromising?"

"Oh, I hope."

"Hope?"

"Hope, because compromise is my friend," Betsy said.

"I'm not sure I..."

"I *live* by compromise. Or in the town next to. I'll be specific. If one tells stories—which I do—compromise is a kind of DNA."

"I think I'm still..."

"Let's say this happened and then that happened and then the other thing happened. Are you following?"

"Possibly."

"A story is, things occur in sequence. C follows B follows A. But sometimes—*sometimes*, depending on who's sitting around the fire—A follows C follows B. You have to compromise. Agreed? You've been married twice—yes?"

"Yes."

"So, what follows what follows what?"

"Again, I'm sorry. I'm not sure—"

"Listen." Betsy Barker announced she'd tell Blake a story. "But before I start, I'm going to say it's a story about my homosexual lawyer son. Where's your head?"

"Where's my head?"

"*Attention*. Erase *head*. Your *attention*. I say what I say, you must have certain expectations. I say it's a story about my homosexual lawyer son. Where's your head?"

"It's...I suppose it's...I'm interested." Blake thought he felt his hair tighten at the back of his skull. "I'm interested," he repeated.

"In what?"

"Well, in..."

"C'mon. This should be easy."

"Well, I suppose *you*. Mostly in you. Because, I mean, we've met. Just. And I'm learning. So mostly you. Then, because children are important, your son. Learning about—but your take. Your part in that—being he's homosexual."

"And so, what if, in the story, I say he has AIDS."

"I'll feel badly. Again, for you."

"What if I say his *partner* has AIDS?"

"Why don't you just tell me the story?"

"What if I say *I* have AIDS?"

Calls erupted outside—throaty, rattling birdcalls. "Sandhills," Blake identified.

"Sand—?"

"Hills. Sandhills. I'd say, let's go outside and I can show them to you, but I can't. It's too dark. And they're too far away."

"Still, let's go outside, anyway," Betsy said. She laughed, then took a sip of her wine. She kept the glass tipped, a small bowl over her upper lip and nose—almost as if she were hiding behind it. "Let's go outside, anyway," she said again, the words a kind of muffled and mossy tumble behind the glass. Her eyes lit.

"I think it's possible you're having me on," Blake said.

"It is. It's possible that I'm having you on. Because having others on is what storytellers do." And, with that, Betsy Barker rose, extended her hand. "Let's go outside, anyway," she said a third time. "We'll go outside. We'll stand in the night. I'll tell you the story I've promised. And I'll tell you the secret behind triplets—repeating the same thought or phrase three times."

"Like the AIDS question."

"Precisely. And like the invitation to—regardless—go outside."

They went outside. The moon was an old moon, paring itself, night by night, away. Perhaps it was the sound of doors—opening, closing—but the sandhills paused for a moment or so, then began again, soon joined by counterpointed voices.

"Swans," Blake identified. "Trumpeters."

"So we have the woodwind and brass sections," Betsy said.

"We left the music *for* the music," Blake said. "We left the music *for* the music. We left the music *for* the music. Is that a triplet? I have season tickets to my own orchestra." He laughed—laughed and rattled on; he couldn't help himself. Gesturing into the night—in directions he knew were too dark for her to follow—he told of what he'd done to refigure the stream, unearth the original bed-gravel, rip the Russian thistle from the embankments, restore the ponds, replant the fields with flax.

"My lord! My lord!" Betsy Barker said.

"My lord," Blake added. Then, "Triplet."

Betsy laughed. "What an extraordinary man," she said. And then, almost in a whisper, "What an extraordinary love you must have. For this place. This home of…what? Earth and water."

They stood. Considering.

"Extraordinary," she finally said. "Triplet with variations."

Blake breathed in, breathed out, thanked her.

They moved to chairs on the front porch and Betsy told her story. In it, her lawyer son and his partner had lived through a winter in which seven of their gay friends had been lost to HIV. To absorb the grief, the two partners, who lived within the D.C. Beltway, had taken a spring trip to the West. One of the friends they'd lost had spoken rapturously about Redfish Lake in Stanley, so they'd rented a cabin there. "It was, in its way, a honeymoon," Betsy said. When they arrived, they couldn't help but notice all the defoliated and fallen conifers in the area. When they asked, they were told, "The pine beetle."

All night long, Betsy said, in their log cabin, the two men held each other and wept. They had left the blight to travel to the blight. The next morning, when they hiked to the lodge for breakfast, it was impossible not to note an almost crimson tinge on the water. When they asked, they were told, "The salmon are back." The lake was called Redfish Lake because, at one point, thousands of coho returned from the ocean to spawn. Word was, you could walk across the lake on their backs. And then dams were built; return denied; abundance faded. But now! Changes had been made. Access had been returned. Redfish Lake was again *Redfish Lake.*

Her son and her son's partner wept again, again held each other. They committed to adopting a child. There was the pine beetle and there was life-renewal. They wept and chose life-renewal. "And that's the story of my homosexual lawyer son," Betsy said.

When she turned, finally, to Blake in the dark, his hand was over his chest.

"Are you all right?" she asked.

"I think so," he said.

"Maybe the steak was too rare," she said.

"Fish, I think, always trump red meat," he said. He felt tired and a bit fragile. "I think I'm going to turn in," he said.

"Keep on turning," Betsy said.

"Fleetwood Mac," Blake said.

Betsy laughed. "Well—how about that? I'm impressed."

The next morning, they found milk, dry cereal, and toast. Blake brewed coffee. "Not exactly IHOP," he said.

"Hey, I'm a cheap date," Betsy said. She wore layered woolens, tweeds, a vest.

"Before I went to bed, I made a couple of calls," Blake said. "About your car. I think I've found the right person."

He had. Before noon—with rewiring and slight alternator modifications—the Focus hummed. When Betsy asked for damages, the mechanic, Jared, said, "I'm cool. I'll eventually get it from this guy—one way or the other." He nodded toward Blake.

"So're you off?" Blake asked Betsy.

"Storytellers try to never be off," Betsy said. "The dream, in fact, of any storyteller is to be *on*. So, of course, now I have to ask: How've I been? Off? On?"

"Oh, on, pretty much, I think," Blake said, and asked if she'd like to spend another night.

"Another compromising night?" she grinned. "Should I check with your families? One? Both? Maybe the present one, at least?"

"Well…end of the day," Blake began wistfully, "I think, maybe *I'm* my family. I'm what you see and get. All there is. So, sure, check with me. I say yes."

"Where can we buy vegetables, then?" Betsy asked. "It's past noon. You let me loose in the vegetables, we'll go back to the ranch, I'll make the best salad you ever had. Then, I think, it'll be time for a nap. Did I see kalamatas in your fridge? Nevermind. I did. And I saw olive oil. And lemons. I'm a spy."

At a farmers market, Betsy bought kale, kohlrabi, cabbage, chard, daikon radishes, avocadoes, and a small sausage of locally made salami. She also bought a new floppy hat. An hour later, everything Betsy had promised would come to pass had, and they were seated on the ranch's back porch, plates in hand, each with a beer sitting on the deck.

"This salad's incredible," Blake said.

"It's the best salad you ever had," Betsy—holding up two fingers—said.

"It is," Blake said. "Not kidding. It's the best salad I ever had." And he held up three.

"The trick's the salami," Betsy said.

A half-hour later, they were taking naps.

When they woke, Blake offered to give Betsy a tour. She said nothing would delight her more.

"Put your new hat on," Blake said. "Fair skin like yours—afternoon sun can do a job on you."

"Direct sun and I are sworn enemies," Betsy said. "Have been forever."

Blake fired up his Yamaha Rhino, and, buckled in, they headed off. He'd brought a folder of enlargements—aerial and other photographs—to show what the property had been when he'd bought it. What they recorded was an expanse of barren, trodden, flat, cattle-grazing land that went on and on and was, essentially, undifferentiated. In all of the images, the stream was arrow-straight and stripped of bankside vegetation so that the cattle had free access to the water. "The whole acreage, for maybe—I don't know—thirty years, had been about raising stock," Blake said.

He showed her where and how they'd given the acreage contour. He walked her along irrigation canals, and explained, best he could, the master plan. He walked her around the rims of restored ponds. "This is where the trumpeter are coming back finally." He pointed. "See, over there's a nest. Down the bank about two hundred feet, another. And you heard last night we're getting sandhills, hundreds of sandhills."

He drove her to fast and slow-moving stretches and explained how the stream had been "re-bent" to follow its originally carved course. He waded in and scooped up gravel. "This was here!" he called. "Who knows how long! The original bed—that got covered over with cow shit and mud." He talked about fish populations and how most had essentially quadrupled since he'd taken the ranch on. "Natives, browns, brookies. Whitefish—but I guess you feed the homeless," he said.

When they were returning, Betsy asked, "So, okay, this is going to sound stupid, but would you call yourself a conservationist?"

"Well—no question I get *called* a conservationist," Blake said. "Especially by local ranchers. But—even as an insult—it always seemed a pretentious word. Still…sure, go ahead, feel free, tell your friends back in…where did you say?"

"Clyde. Clyde, North Carolina."

"Clyde, North Carolina—that you spent two nights with a conservationist. Or conservationalist—that's even better. Conservationalista! Make it sound political. It'll make a good story."

There was a red Jeep Comanche parked outside the garage when they got back.

"Visitor?" Betsy asked.

"Oldest son, from my first marriage," Blake explained. "Luke."

Luke, tan and muscular and in his early forties, sat on the back porch drinking a Fat Bastard ale and reading *Outside Magazine*. Blake made introductions. Luke seemed disinterested. "You've had some cutthroat jumping," Luke said. "A couple—pretty decent size."

"We're still getting mid-afternoon, late-afternoon hatches," Blake returned. "Still warm enough, not too cold."

Blake brought out two more beers and tried engineering a three-way conversation—chumming it with the story of Betsy's failed Focus. Luke only made body sounds and went back to his *Outside*. A half-hour into talk that was, at best, stilted, the rumble of an approaching SUV broke any semblance of conversation. The rumbling stopped; the engine cut.

"More family?" Betsy asked. It was the sister of Blake's present wife and her thirteen-year-old daughter. Again, introductions. The sister-in-law's name was Onnie; the daughter's, Shel. Onnie got herself a beer, Shel got herself a Diet Coke, and they joined the porch gathering.

"People come, people go," Blake said, offering a shrug. "Less, though, now. October. I tell them, *You need a break? Come up. Use the ranch.*"

"You're a generous soul," Betsy said.

"Maybe. Maybe not."

"Not maybe."

"Maybe, then."

"Oh—are we interrupting something?" Onnie asked.

"Uncle Blake? Can I catch fish from your dock with your net?" Shel asked.

Luke rose and moved with his Fat Bastard and copy of *Outside* to the far end of the porch.

Blake lifted from his Adirondack rocker. "If you'll excuse me. Relax, get to know one another. Hatch is on, I'm heading off to fish."

"Would you like me to—?" Betsy began.

"She's a wonderful storyteller." Blake nodded at Betsy. "Maybe you can get her to tell one. Ask her about triplets."

"Oh, do you have triplets?" Onnie asked.

Betsy's voice stumbled, trailed her host. "Blake—if you'd like company—"

But the screen to the deck was shutting and Blake was off the porch.

"So that's true? You're a storyteller?" Onnie asked.

"If called upon," Betsy said.

"You mean like...professionally?"

When Blake got back hours later, he could hear voices outside. The sun was low and had all the citrine intensity and density of a gemstone. Blake poured some Knob Creek over ice and began cleaning the four trout he'd caught—wondering, as he gutted and rinsed them—what four such disparate people had ever found to talk about. It occurred to him that it wasn't four voices he was hearing; it was one. A single voice taking parts, and the voice was Betsy's.

Blake slipped the cleaned trout into Ziplocs and set them in the fridge. If another person would cook, they'd have trout for dinner. When he turned from the fridge, though, he saw Betsy's overnight bag parked on the floor by the front door. Coming in, he'd missed it. Suddenly he was angry—angry at his son, and at his wife's sister and her spoiled daughter. They'd upset an October day that had been a sweet connecting for him. Betsy'd said she spend one more night—but no; she wasn't.

From the porch screen, he could see Betsy—in an Adirondack by the stairs. The others, in smaller chairs, faced her. She'd donned her new floppy hat and one of his fishing vests and was bent forward telling her story. He didn't interrupt, only stood and listened as her voice rose and fell, as her hands moved in the slightest of air currents—like fish biding time in a holding pool. Eyes sometimes wide, sometimes closed as if straining to remember, she went on.

"But after twelve years, I think of us as bugs on the surface of the water," she said, paused, continued. "No—not on the surface, *in* it, within that line of demarcation…not air, not water…sometimes submerged, sometimes not." Betsy saw him, winked. "You have watched an unbreaking groundswell in a cove," she picked up. "The water shallow, the cove quiet, a little sinister with satiate familiarity, while beyond the darkling horizon the dying storm has raged, raged on. That was the water, we the flotsam," she announced. "Even after twelve years, it is no clearer than that. It had no beginning and no ending. Out of nothing we howled."

Then, the others leaning in, Betsy stopped. "I'm sorry," she said. "That's going to have to be it. Far as I'm able to go." She smiled at Blake standing on the other side of the door. "How's the fisherman?" she asked. Then, before he could answer, explained, "I was telling them William Faulkner's *The Bear*. My version—his words. I got as far as I could. But with an early morning flight, I need to skedaddle."

"Didn't you tell me—?"

"That was pretty amazing," Luke said.

"I'm not sure I understood it—but you had me," Onnie said.

"I didn't understand *any* of it—but I loved it," Shel said.

"Well, usually a good story tells itself," Betsy said. She stood, removed Blake's vest, then shook her hands as if she'd just pulled them from dishwater. "Loosening up for the long drive," she said, then looked at Blake still standing on the far side of the porch screen. "Sir?"

"Sorry to have missed the story," Blake said.

"Next time," Betsy said. She extended goodbyes, shook hands, pulled Luke in close. "You look like you need a hug," she said.

Blake walked with her, carrying the overnight to her car. "Sorry about the intrusions," he said.

"Life intrudes," Betsy said.

"Life's fine. I like life. It's the people," Blake said.

"I intruded," Betsy said. "So I thought best I leave."

"You never intruded," Blake said.

"Life instructs, then," Betsy said. "Or maybe *intrudes* and *instructs* are anagrams. Maybe."

Her overnight was in the trunk; the trunk shut. The two stood by the driver's door. Blake looked sad. Betsy was smiling. Head up, hat tickling her shoulder blades, she moved into him. "C'mere you big ol' conservationalist!" she said. She wrapped around him. "Give me a hug," she said. "Give me a big, long hug."

And he did.

Into the shoulder of his Patagonia vest, she said, "Here are some more words from William Faulkner. Now listen up. *Gratitude is a quality similar to electricity: it must be produced and discharged and used up in order to exist at all.*"

"I'm not sure I understand that," Blake said.

"Nor me," Betsy said.

He watched her Ford Focus diminish, then fade down the dirt entry road until he was only watching a rooster tail of dust. "Drive carefully, it's a long journey," he said to the late afternoon.

A month later, on an early November day, Blake was back, retreating again to his ranch. When he opened the freezer for some kind of piecemeal breakfast—maybe frozen waffles—he discovered his four trout in their Ziplocs. They looked suspended between life in the stream and the hope they provided of nourishment.

He pulled them out, set them on the sinkside granite, wishing that someone who knew how to cook trout were there to prepare and cook them. Maybe he could smoke them; he knew the smoker. If he smoked them, then the chill air and his own lungs would bear their taste for at least an hour. And that would be a nice memory. A memory. A nice one.

THE FISH MAGICIAN

1.

Malcolm hears the call, the invitation, and rises from his seat, his wife Ginger's hand like a heat phantom floating in the air behind him—pushing him forward? Staying him? It's hard to tell. Malcolm climbs the stairs, mounts the stage, says hello to the thin magician, shakes his hand, steps into a box windowed by Lucite, pinned by light. And—seeing the man with the cape unfurl something huge and purple, something velveteen, up and into the air over the box (if there is sound—sound hushed), then seeing no more, seeing nothing because seeing leaps beyond vision, becomes gem-color before anything's seen, some essential ardor of emerald, ruby, some hard-color truth in a gale wind that sucks every bone into his breath. Malcolm feels himself hurled then hurled—somewhere North, off the stage, out of the theater, casino, resort: out of town finally, across one state line, possibly two, where it smells like juniper, a thousand edgeless rocks, heron feathers. One imagines Idaho. Why not? A sign, print burned into wood then stained, says Magic Reservoir. Why not. Malcolm listens for clues and hears only a world beyond traffic.

2.

All I ever wanted to be was funny. But fate deals. They call sports the gateway into whatever you'd do if you had brains or talent. I was a second-string All American, playing four years with the Cincinnati Bengals, four more with the San Diego Chargers. Truth's funny when you say it right. And we get second chances. So, funny was what I tried to be, broadcasting

Monday Night Football with the Wildebeest and the Prince of Nose Candy, but the network saw what I thought hilarious differently, told me shut up or leave. Be reasonable. How does a broadcaster shut up? So I left, made a little noise, went on talk shows for a year—did you know Boomer Esiason?—nevermind—got sued twice, run down by a car (not an accident), body knocked into a ditch in a remote, Saskatchewan I-think-the-word-is-village. For a week I was the missing body. But then I regained, what I've realized since then, more than consciousness, found myself, climbed up onto the road, got found, came here, and now do what I do: try to employ my more-than-consciousness, find other people, audition, do the comedy clubs.

True story: I'm taking lunch at the Mirage California Pizza Kitchen so I can watch the Sportsbook with a pair of hundred-power Bushnells, and this woman comes up—handsome, mid-forties, jewelry, nicely accessorized—asks am I who I am? Is my casebook full? Good, because she has a missing body.

The missing body's her husband. They went to see Lance Burton at the Monte Carlo last night. *Great show!* she said. *Great show! Have you seen it?* Of course. *Somewhere around*—she looked at her watch—*10:46, Lance asks for someone in the audience.* Woman's husband's a magic freak, been one since he was a kid, pops up out of his showroom seat, goes up, steps into the box; Lance makes him disappear, does seven other tricks, levitates himself on a motorcycle, roadtrips the air—blue smoke.

The show ends, the theater empties. My lady's waiting, waiting. She's the only one in the theater= except a stagehand; he says, *Ma'am*? She says, *Lance Burton made my husband—my husband, Malcolm—disappear. Where would he—?* Stagehand has no idea. *Wait here*, he says. It's five, ten, fifteen minutes. Man comes out in a suit, looks very casino. *Would you come with me*, he asks. My lady follows; the two go into an office. Clearly executive, clearly management; office is like a suite, full bar, entertainment center. *What would you like to drink?* the executive asks. *Any piroshki? Dolmathes?* She repeats her story. *Where's my husband?*

Sit down, the executive suit says. *Please. I need to explain something.* But first he makes her sign a paper saying all he tells her will be in strictest confidence.

She does. As much of a suit as the executive is, the guy is shaking; he's a man probably plays golf six out of seven and he's white. *Something tragic is happening,* he says. Lance Burton—one of the great magicians of the world and for whom the Monte Carlo built and designed their present showroom—is losing his memory. *Hands are fine*, executive says. *Skill's as nimble as ever. The man defines 'dexterous.' Short term, though, is another matter.*

Where's my husband? my lady asks.

We wish we knew, executive says. He'd asked Lance. *Lance, you remember making the gentleman in the black turtleneck, brown houndstooth disappear?*

Lance said yes.

So, do you remember where you disappeared him to?

Trust me: Lance feels terrible. He feels humiliated. He knows this is happening to him. And I have to tell you, it's unforgiving. It's cruel. One of the great magicians of the world.

Where does Lance disappear most of his things, most of the people? What my lady'd been told was, *Different places.*

Like?

Apparently, there's no pattern. That was part of Lance's fun. Sometimes the ballroom of the MGM. *The further away, the more the challenge*, is what Lance had said. And in the last year—almost to defy loss of memory—he'd pushed. One time he'd made a horse disappear and the horse showed up onstage with Rosie O'Donnell in Atlantic City. My lady had asked around, and I had a certain infamy for missing bodies. She'd read a hack piece in *Sports Illustrated* about the network firing me and how that had led, in ways, to me finding missing bodies. The Monte Carlo would pay. Would I talk to Lance? Would I take the case?

One of the funniest books in the Old Testament, I think, is Job. His boils kill me. It cracks me up how Job says, *Let the night be solitary*. How do you come up with a line like that? Job's like Chaplin, he's like this ancient little tramp who can't get anything; it's a riot. Chapter ten is comic genius. Verse ten: *Hast thou not poured me out as milk, curdled me like cheese?* I mean, it's just one of those things that's funny—same way Wisconsin is funny. Except I would have ended Job differently. Cut chapter forty-two, had it end where the darts are counted as stubble and he's laughing at a shaking spear. I'm working up a whole Job routine. I wouldn't mind being a warm-up at the Monte Carlo.

So I say yes. *Have the Monte Carlo call Lance. Also, have them agree: the missing body in return for one night in Lance's Evening of Magic.*

Do you have even an intuition? my lady asks. I see fields of mission bells, bitterroot. *Idaho*, I say.

Idaho? she puzzles. *But there's no connection. We have no connection whatsoever with Idaho, we've never been there.*

All the more reason for the intuition, I say.

Lance is at a loss when, over the phone, I take him through guided imagery. His voice sags on all the unaccented syllables. He tries. Still, he comes up with postcards: lava rock, watercress, a blue heron. *I'm missing a dove,* he tells me, *a small water fountain...half an assistant.*

I'll keep my eyes out, I tell him. A dove, a small fountain, half an assistant—lava rock, watercress, a blue heron. I take the elevator to the top of the Stratosphere, walk around the observation. I call my lady, whose name is Ginger. *Any word?* I ask. Before Ginger can answer, the second cell I'd forgotten in my pocket rings. Ginger hears it, says, *Any chance it's Malcolm?* It's the Monte Carlo, seeing if she's still in town, but I don't say that.

I take a cab up the Boulevard, walk around backstage, am let into the Magic Room, touch boxes, blades of swords, birdcages. *Idaho!* everything whispers—like sex, like the relics of saints—*Idaho!* There are three blood-carpeted stairs to a small platform; I climb them. I disappear, just for a moment, then reappear. My breathing's shallow, rock-washed, filled with ozone. I leave the Magic Room, call Ginger. *Meet me at Sfuzzi's,* I say. *Seven o'clock, in the Fashion Mall. It's across from the Dive.*

I root out Ginger's executive—a man with sunken eyes, sunken cheeks, and a nose that's listing. I say, *Mr. Castelli, I need an hour with Lance.*

Castelli's voice wants to scramble my signal. He's all distrust pretending to be cooperation. He says, *I guess, okay, if a lawyer's present. But don't get any ideas; you're going to have to prove magical negligence.*

Lance Burton's by his pool, with a lawyer. The air's sheeted like phyllo; light's like lava rock. *Make something disappear*, I say. I'm just trying to find a handle. *It doesn't have to be difficult; anything.*

He chooses the water in the pool. It's gone; the pool's dry, then it's back again.

Interesting, I say. *Do it again. Something else.* He's wearing a bathing suit with fish. The fish disappear, it's a solid blue suit; then the rainbows are back again. *One more time*, I request. He's eating a salad. He waves his hand, and that's the end of the watercress; it's just radicchio. *You're good*, I say. That's the word on the street and I can't dispute it. *Bring the watercress back.*

Bring the what back? Lance Burton says, and the lawyer whispers something into his ear.

We do word association and it might as well be sandblasting. I say *coriander*; he says *sigmoidoscopy*. I ask has he ever seen Malcolm prior to last night—in videotape, perhaps, photograph? And prior conversations with Malcolm's Ginger?

The Monte Carlo lawyer leans in, whispers. *We take exception to your implications*, he says. *Mr. Burton's no hit magician.*

Except he is a hit magician, I say, and though it's reasonably quick, it's not funny.

I meet Ginger at Sfuzzi's. When the hostess asks inside or outside, I say, *It's the story of my life.*

Ginger prefers inside—where she feels more volume, she says, more shape. They have conditioner ducts the color of jicama. We split an *insalata mista* and I order a bottle of Marilyn Merlot—you take your laughs wherever.

What've you found? Ginger asks, and on this particular night—full moon, Strip traffic like gelatin, the sound of the Dive next door hitting the bottom of the ocean—*What've you found?* seems such a delicious question.

I have a theory about inevitability. Greek tragedy used to be comedy before it was tragedy. The House of Atreus was originally a funhouse—something happened to the mirrors; Sophocles broke one, then figured *fuckit*, broke them all. Discoveries used to be marriages before they were blindings; people spilled wine, not blood; professional football used to be professional magic before special teams. It's the mirror thing all over—again and again. Back at the beginning, fish had feathers.

Ginger had merlot on her upper lip, the unwashed crust of a crying jag on one cheekbone. Bodies get lost—isn't that amazing?—but not forever. That you can find the missing body again and again is, I think, a miracle. What had I found out?

It's indisputable, I say.

What's indisputable?

Idaho.

Idaho's indisputable?

Absolutely.

How can Idaho be indisputable?

You're wild, Ginger.

Seriously.

Because, look at us. Look at where we are.

Yes, she says.

Smell the night, I say.

She does.

I say, *Idaho's the next state.*

3.

Malcolm supports himself against a lodgepole at the foot of the spillway. *I was somewhere*, he thinks. *Somewhere in a world not here—where was that?* Folded on the stones are his black turtleneck, brown houndstooth. There are plovers, stellar jays on branches. Indigo buntings browse the ground thatch: seeds? With each inquiry of beak: seeds? seeds? The water falling sounds like applause.

Where was it that he...? Memory, in this place, seems very much like a binnacle in a kitchen in Oklahoma—a thing unnecessary. Malcolm thinks, *The inevitability of water! Comedy of light!* He forgoes connections—because there are open birdcages in a logjam of tamarack and black hawthorn, nesting cinnamon teal, rock dove. There's a small fountain lodged in a listing Engelmann. Colored scarves blow by like sheeting rain. In a field rife with Russian thistle, beyond which horses dance, is half a woman. Upper.

Oh, my dear! Malcolm says.

Hello! the half-woman says. *Take a card, any card! My name's Sheila!*

What happened? Malcolm says.

Isn't this all wonderful? Sheila says. *Finally? At last?*

But you're only half here, Malcolm says.

At least I'm half here, Sheila says. Then, *Look! Oh, look!* and points, and a purple cape floats by on the Big Wood River.

Two others, man and woman, climb the horizon of barbed wire, up over what seems a stairway and down; the man overburdened with sinew and lank, the woman's wrists mirrors of atmosphere. Between them, a picnic basket and a boom box. The boom box plays Kenny G.

Ginger! Malcolm says.

Idaho! Ginger says.

The lank man, wishing he could be funny, points behind to a small ladder where the two had climbed.

Sportsman's Access, he says. *It says Magic Reservoir Sportsman's Access.*

WALKING TOWARD BOISE

A man holds an axe over the neck of a boy. Or perhaps it's not an axe; it just looks like an axe. Possibly it's a baseball bat. The man, a father, offering the handle to his son, the bat having somehow trapped a blade of late afternoon light. How do we know, finally, what's dangerous? Maybe what we see is a field trip—teacher with butterfly net, student watching, net in the air over the student's head. And what seems the white head of an axe is only cheesecloth. Or perhaps a man's hand—fingers slick and glistening with water. Why couldn't the man be a man of God and the terrible scene a baptism?

What is it in us that pursues transgression—seeks cruelty and assumes the Old Testament? Certainly, there is a man. And a boy, certainly. And, yes: something in the air over the boy's head—an object, burnished enough to reflect. But this is the very beginning of our story—*Once upon a time a man and a boy*—we don't know any more. We're not close enough. We've been here, what—a minute?

The world stands in, often, for itself. We pull up a raincoat around our neck when it should be a blanket. Where there should be a car sitting in a driveway, there's an old refrigerator. Should we expect the refrigerator to rev its engine and back over the border collie in the driveway standing in for the pit bull that the family really wanted but was afraid of?

We leap ahead because we see only partially. Hungry to know, we fill details in—cruel father, trusting son. If we can't assemble a true story, we'll construct a ghost story and call it true.

First, though, let's simply stand and watch. Move in: move

closer. The axe, if it is an axe, is lowered. The man kneels before the boy, takes his shoulders. Says something. The boy's head drops briefly—then lifts and seems to look straight into the face of the man.

Is the man angry? Is he telling the boy of the boy's inadequacies—how stupid he is? How he loses things? How he never meets a single request properly? Hard to tell. So we lean in to hear whether the wind carries anger—but none comes. Again, what we can't escape: close as we are, it's not close enough. So we move again—trying, at the same time, to diminish distance and elude connection.

Trying to diminish distance and elude connection—be there and not if possible, a crucial part of events but, at the same time, removed; involved but never implicated.

There's a line somewhere, somewhere in the dust (if we can find the dust) which—if we can avoid crossing it, stay on our own side—will keep us safe. Will allow us to see, finally, if the axe is an axe, if what we're party to is sacrifice or baptism, if the head of the child is, finally, blessed or severed from the child's neck. And if there's blood, does it bloom or spill and ball in the loose earth like some black and hallowed gravel?

If we measure, get close enough, we can know if this is a world we would want to claim or one to walk away from. Because the person we're trying to save, finally, in any story, is our self.

Imagine a different place. Speak of a theater. Speak of a stage; speak of a magician on it. In fact, make him the autobiography's famous Blue Magician, place him in his own favorite chapter, "Bringing the Tricks Home," and have him make the apparent unapparent.

Too easy. No. Have him make the unapparent apparent. In a reach, have him invade the air precisely where he's revealed nothing exists, and have there—theatricalized by light, scored by autoharp—*be* something. And then: something times two! Times three! Four! Oh, the melodrama of magic!

See! Hear! A bevy of doves. A dozen cigarettes. *Hello-Goodbye!* The Blue Magician directs; the Blue Magician instructs: *Nothing…nothing…watch!* And, of course, we watch. Watch and watch and watch. It's hard to exhaust our watching when something out of nothing is possible.

We want to please and answer to the Voice. We do. We want to be the object if the object's love. A man with a strap in his hands says *do this*, we obey—especially if the man's named Our Father. In a sense, we can't suffer *enough* if he will just remain Our Father. Like the sacred elk—we'll walk into the archer's arrow, even say *thank you*—to have it some kind of meeting framed by blood. I say a man; I say a boy—but it's all transparent.

The human moment is irresistible. At any given instant, we feel responsible for more human moments, almost, than we can bear. We have either made mistakes or been the instruments of mistakes far too many times. Any more—more error, regret—and we will give way, nearly, under the weight. And yet—! We struggle from our knees. Stand. Come back for more. Because we're curious. Because we want, sometimes, more than anything, to be dead center at our own punishments.

So, with this scene, trying, still, to test closeness without connection, we edge closer. Somewhere, someone's said *the whole thing's details*. Exposure of a neck, dilation of an eye, position of a tongue against teeth. *Learn as much as you can*, we've been instructed. Not everything. Never everything—but *as much as possible.*

And what we see, when we edge closer—beyond the boy's obvious Obsidian Little League T-shirt, man's white dress shirt and loosened tie—is that the boy's eyes look, at once, frightened, curious, and sad. That the man's neck looks carved. We look around for the instrument, the axe, don't see one. Something's there, though, on the ground. Flat. Not an axe—a baseball bat. Which could be dangerous or not. Father? Son?

How well have we read this? We sense the man's anything but a stranger to the boy. Which doesn't mean either one is out of danger.

My own father—after attempted suicide and a year away from his own death—framed an empty space in the room as we were talking and said, *She was hanging there.*

She was hanging there? What? What is she? But, of course, I know: his mother. She was hanging there, immigrant woman without a husband, and two sons on the Lower East Side and it had become, all of it, too much. And he—the man, my father—had come home from school to discover she'd hanged herself. For him there were no fathers and sons, no permanent man and boy. He would have lowered his neck for the axe—I believe that. *I* would have. But neither of us, really, were asked to. And if there's a sacrifice, if there's a tragedy, that may be it.

Here's some help. Here's the scene which took place ten minutes before the scene we've happened upon. Someone else caught it on videotape, and though it's undeveloped, the scene's there. Someone will press PLAY at a future point, and it will unroll. Others will watch.

Help, then. PLAY, then.

Same place. Outside. Unmowed grass. Dandelions. Rocks. Igneous from two-million-year-old volcanoes. House in the background. Late afternoon light. Same, same. For the most part, always. Except the boy is holding the baseball bat; it's not on the ground. And except—see?—there's a woman wearing a down vest. Red. Stitched white. And there's a blue Adidas bag in her hand. Caught on the video camera, she's crying. Her face is twisted like amphibian skin. Eyeliner smeared. Eyes like a nest of worms.

The man, like us, is trying to edge closer. The boy is backing away. The woman's swinging the blue Adidas bag at the man—saying between her teeth, *Asshole! Asshole! Get away!* And he's saying, *Baby, baby, please! Please, this isn't the time.* And the boy is saying, *Mama! Don't!* So we have the sense now that the boy is the man's son; the man, the boy's father. *Mama—please!*

On the videotape, the Adidas bag catches the man at the side of his unkempt head and he wavers backwards, trips over a rock, falls, hits the base of his skull on another rock, tries to scramble to his feet, loses balance, stumbles, falls again, moves his hand to the back of his head, brings it away, discovers blood.

So this is a story threatened by blood, as it first appeared. It has an immanence of some kind, a danger. Pain, anger, frustration: somebody feeling someone else wrong and reacting.

Baby—come inside, we'll talk, we hear on the audiotape. The man.

Right! we hear.

Please.

Mama—

Right—and talk and talk. And nothing ever changes.

I've told you, change takes time.

Right. Like the birth and death of a star.

So now we know: the woman knows about certain things. Stars.

Please, Mama, we hear.

Jess, I'm sorry.

Dora—please! The man rises to his feet. He puts a hand up to his neck, tears the top button of his shirt open, loosens his tie. *Don't act rashly*, he says. *Don't do something you—*

Don't act rashly, she shouts back.

I'm serious.

Easy for you to say!

Dora—

Dell—I need to get away from you!

Fine. But what about the boy?

Right now, I can't worry about—

Dora, you're his mother.

Right, and you're his father.

Now we've confirmed something. And, although we may not like it, we at least feel clear.

How are you going to—?

I don't know!

Please! You don't have any—

Dell—I'll find a way!

We see the boy drop the baseball bat, try to stand on it as it rolls under him, under his feet on the ground. We think, *Why is he doing that?* It's crazy: trying to stand on a bat, stand on a thing that rolls when his mother and father are yelling at each other. We see him fall. We see the man looking at his hand, at the blood there. We see the woman head off, screaming, *I'm leaving and walking toward Boise! Whatever happens on the road'll be better than everything that's been—*

We see the man staring at his hand as if it's stopped being his hand, as if it's a death notice. We see the boy on his hands and knees in the grass like a dog. We hear him bark. Hear him barking and barking—his mother disappearing out of the frame of the video camera, setting out, presumably, for Boise.

We see the father unable to stop looking at the blood on his hand. We move closer to the monitor, and see that the father's hand is webbed together, like the foot of a swan or goose. Webbed in blood.

The scene doesn't change—father looking at his hand, boy barking on all fours, mother gone from the frame—for a full minute.

And that's all it appears we'll know. Though we can always imagine. Because by the time the video tape runs out—and the father drops his blood-stitched hand to his side, son rises to his knees, and we look back again at the scene that compelled our attention in the first place—man and boy are gone, mother, distant.

Something stirs the air. Voices trying to climb over one another and falling back, awkward as puppies, like a brood of kit fox. Voices trying to clean and nurse one another in a tumble:

tongue and mouth. Each voice—when we hear it, when we can untangle it from the clamor, is saying, *I'm sorry. I'm sorry. Please, I'm sorry. I'm sorry. I'm sorry—*

The three—mother, father, son—appear. They're trying to do the impossible: move ahead and hold one another at the same time. *Sorry, please, I'm sorry. I'm sorry.*

This is a difficult world to agree to. To see closely enough and say *yes* in. This is a difficult world in which to, finally, love. So, draw impossibly close. See as much as you're able. And, if you can, find a story without demarcation.

IDAHO

For Patrick, at thirty-six, distance is crucial. An inevitable sadness. For him, truly powerful love involves separation—the love-object across a continent. Better yet: a sea. Love next door seems prosaic.

Love at a distance began when, as an undergraduate in Corvallis, Oregon, he fell in love with a young Louisiana Tech veterinary student named Vallery. They'd struck up a conversation at a Citgo along I-40 in southern Colorado and exchanged addresses. For two and a half years, they corresponded and imagined a life together, swapped pictures of manatees for prints of Nolde. Telephone calls collapsed into crying jags or silences.

Then, during the first year of architectural school in San Diego, Patrick met Helena, a botanist from Barre, Vermont and eight years older. She was with her niece and nephew whom she'd taken to Sea World, and they were standing in line for an Abba concert. Patrick loved saying, *I met a woman from Barre; she's remarkable.* They spent four years burning favorite-artist CDs for one another and experimenting with their own form of phone sex: *Light a match. Stare into the flame. Tell me what it is you see. Tell me about the shoes in your closet. If I were a piece of underwear, what piece of underwear would I be?*

Then there was the Taos-Ashville romance followed by the Vail-Key West affair. Love and distance. Patrick had never actually crossed an ocean, though the opportunity, once, had been there. For the last three years and just ending, it had been Durant, Oklahoma and Gulfport, Louisiana—himself and Claire. Claire was a photographer and painter who captured disasters—fires and storms. Hurricane Katrina made her famous and the fame had somehow made her bold. "Come for my opening, and afterwards we'll fuck on the beach," she'd demanded in an email.

Patrick suggested, instead, that—after her opening—she fly west and they meet in Idaho.

"What do you mean—*Idaho*?" Claire had said.

"I mean Idaho," Patrick had said. "As in River of No Return and the Grand Tetons." He announced that she'd love Idaho and that she and Idaho were like one another—wet and gemlike and powerful.

"Don't be an asshole," Claire had said. And that—just two weeks before—had been the end.

Idaho stayed, though, as a notion, as a place far enough away for love to happen.

It's a Tuesday in October, and Patrick is restless and hoping for release from Claire. Idaho's far. Idaho's over a thousand miles—still potential, possible—so Patrick climbs into his new Explorer and aims there. For two days, he plays and replays Keith Jarrett's *La Scala,* Jarrett's notes sounding at once overly determined and free. *Architecture is frozen music*, Patrick thinks. Someone had said that. And isn't music architecture?

He passes a semi tumbled into the thatched median. Fire trucks flank it. Ambulances. The cab is in flames. People seem to be doing their jobs but not concerned. A heavy equipment driver friend had once told Patrick about drivers he'd pulled from rollovers: "Sometimes, coming out, you'll be totally naked, every inch of skin slick with some guy's blood." That's not this kind of wreck—it doesn't seem a blood wreck. It seems calmer.

October hills of hay roll and fall, roll again. Patrick thinks the word *ocean*. He thinks other words, images: *salt marshes, wading birds, oyster beds.* He begins counting fence posts, redwings. Stops. *What am I counting?* he asks.

Utah now, and he passes Bear River, Snowville. He loves the names of towns. Fire, water, earth. Animals. Elements.

So, okay, it's over—himself and Claire. She's...beyond. Away. Past even the distance of love. But where? Where is she? Right now—at this moment. In bed? Far away in bed? Sleeping? Or perhaps in a bath, gelling herself, making her body long, letting it float there, blur, in one of her watercolor moves of mood. Or perhaps she's eating oysters—even, perhaps, settled in with a more convenient lover. Unwashed skin on skin.

"You have this need for a secret life," Patrick's ex-wife, Elaine, once said. "You want to be wherever you can't be, and with people you shouldn't be with."

True? Perhaps. He had an appetite. A disconnected hunger. For what?

Pocatello, the sign reads.

So what kind of a name is Pocatello? Indian? Should he stay on I-15, then, to Pocatello? Or switch over to I-84, to Twin Falls?

Patrick chooses Twin Falls. From Twin Falls he can either go on to Boise, feel himself in the capital, or travel north on U.S. 93—up to Hailey, Ketchum, even over Galena Summit to Stanley. Either way, he can embed himself. Like volcanic granite. Pocatello is too close to the border. Patrick doesn't want to feel almost in Utah. That wouldn't be Idaho.

He turns the volume up on the Keith Jarrett, turns it down. He thinks of calling his ex, Elaine, where she works, and announcing: *Not that it matters at this point—but Claire and I are history*. He sees highway signs for Rupert, Burley, Jerome.

"You like that? That Explorer?"

The woman asking at the truck stop north of Twin Falls on 93 appears in her early forties. "I've been thinking of stepping up from this Chevy piece-of-shit 2x4." She's tall—six foot, even—skinny, long mouse-colored hair that—even at fifteen feet and over the gas evaporation—smells of smoke. She wears

Levis, torn at the knees and crotch, where Patrick can make out green silk underwear.

"I like it. It's nice," Patrick says. "It's sturdy. It gets me around."

"Sturdy—gets you around?" the woman says, marking, facial expressions aside, that she doesn't think much of his answer.

"Meets my needs," Patrick explains.

"So, how is it as a screwmobile?" the woman asks. "I like fucking in a car. Or, in my case, a truck. How's it for that?"

"I haven't tried yet," Patrick says. He squeezes the nozzle pump, rounding off his payment.

"Well, you're a dickhead, then, aren't you?" the woman says. "I haven't tried it yet," she mocks. "So then, what *have* you tried with it?"

"Look—" Patrick begins.

"It's not a complicated question," the woman snaps.

"Getting from here to there," Patrick says. "I've tried getting from here to there—and it's fine."

"Oh. Getting from here to there! Well, isn't that a smart thing. Isn't that just the most efficient thing in the world."

"Listen, have a good day," Patrick says, and he moves hurriedly away to buy his gas, get a can of iced tea for the road.

When he gets back, the woman is sitting in his passenger seat. Patrick opens the door. "Okay. You've made your point," he says.

"Hooray for me! And what's my point?" the woman says. "And who's Claire?" She waves Claire's last letter. "And why is she exhausted? You wear her out?"

"Would you like me to call the Highway Patrol?" Patrick asks.

"Jack, hey, lighten up," the woman says.

Patrick swings the passenger door wide.

"I don't get it," the woman says. "Tasty dish like me offers you a freebie—offers you an up-close-and-personal—"

"No accounting for taste," Patrick says.

"Hey, taste me first—*then* say that," the woman says. She slides her long legs so that they dangle out of the car. "You know, you're a sexy-looking man. How come such a sexy-looking man acts like such an asshole? Wild Idaho woman wants to get laid in your Ford Explorer and you tell her to get lost."

Patrick shrugs.The woman slides out. She stands, scopes Patrick—eyes like radiology. "I want to get laid in that Explorer," she says. "I'll also give you a blowjob that'll make your hair stand on end. Why do I think you're an idiot?"

"What can I say," Patrick shrugs.

"Well, you can say *Oh, baby, yes! Yes! Let's break each other's bones! Get back in!*" the woman says.

"Nice talking with you," Patrick says. He shuts the passenger door.

"You going to lock it?" The woman mugs, makes her eyes go wide. "Call your State Farm rep to up your no-touch insurance?"

Patrick moves around to the driver's side.

"You going to see Claire? That who you're going to see? Your exhausted friend? According to the postmark, you're headed in the wrong direction."

"I guess there's always reverse," Patrick says, then slides in.

"So then I still have a chance," the woman says.

"No," Patrick said. And he closes the door.

"Well, I'm going to follow you anyway! And hope!"

He can hear her voice outside. Forewarning. He starts his engine. She bolts to her pickup. He pulls out. She pulls out after him and starts a hazardous tailgating.

Jesus—back off! Patrick thinks.

Once, when Patrick was sad and hapless, he awoke in an out of town room, his sheet matted with blood. He remembers lifting the sheet as though it had been a down feather—something lighter than life, mysterious, even thrilling. The blood on the sheet had seemed so dark. Or was it the sheet? The darkness. There had been a blue disposable razor on the gold Comfort Inn rug. Patrick had felt drunk. From the Jim Beam he'd taken to bed or—? He'd checked his arms—crusty and caked. *Why would I do that?* he'd thought. *Why would a person with an admirable life do that?*

Then, a later time, thinking about Claire, he'd formed the words: *A person lets himself out.* Blood or heart or desire—you let yourself out finally. *You can't stay in.*

"So why do you surrender so often?" Elaine had asked once. "To sadness? Unless that's what you want." She'd gone on, "I can't imagine someone giving in to sadness who doesn't *want* sadness. Sadness seems a choice. You say yes or no. You say, *This is a life I embrace—or not.* I mean, do you *enjoy* the misery? Of what it is you can't help?"

The woman in the ragged Levis and Chevy 2x4 is still tailgating, and Patrick supposes it's her idea of a joke. *Let her have her fun*, he thinks. She'll follow, harass, then grow tired and pull over, turn around, fade to black. She thinks, somehow, she has an advantage—being brassy, pushy. When she can't find any measurable discomfort, she'll give up. Except she's still behind him, twelve miles later, in Shoshone.

Before the railroad tracks and without a signal, Patrick turns. The woman in the Chevy 2x4 banks a hard left, following. Patrick circles the block. The woman circles. In his rearview, he believes he can make her face out, and it's grinning. On his second loop, he notices a sheriff's car parked outside the Shoshone Café, so he pulls in two cars away and checks what the woman might do. She's four or five cars back, in the street, idling.

Patrick gets out, locks his doors, goes into the café, and finds a bulky man in a uniform sitting at the counter eating a bowl of chili. The man looks sour, as if the chili is rancid or as if he needs to arrest someone.

"Officer?" Patrick tries.

The officer lifts a spoon halfway to his mouth, holds the chili, looks at it. The gesture says, *Go away. Can't you see I'm eating?* But, hell, Patrick's started and he can't stop.

"Officer?" he begins again.

The man turns his spoon over, lets the chili slide back into his bowl, stares at the empty spoon. "I'm listening," he says.

"I need a bit of advice, I think," Patrick says.

"About?"

"I have a woman in a Chevy 2x4—"

The officer cuts in: "That'd be LaRelle," he says.

Patrick scrambles.

"Got pushy at some truck stop. Made moves. Right? Crowded you? When you said no—started following you?"

"Exactly," Patrick says.

"Oh, LaRelle!" the officer says.

"So—"

"Pull into the Ice Caves," the officer says into his chili. He hasn't even turned toward Patrick.

"Excuse me?"

"Ten, eleven miles up, you'll see a sign: Shoshone Ice Caves. Go there. In there. LaRelle is a woman of hunger. Anywhere else, she'd dog you till she was satisfied. But she hates the Ice Caves. You turn into the Ice Caves, she'll vamoose. Oh, she might follow—up to the parking lot, maybe, but you pay your fee, go inside, take the left passageway—smaller one—she'll be outta your life forever. That's fine, don't thank me, I love giving advice."

"Thank you."

"You're welcome." And the man slides the spoonful of chili into his mouth.

About seven miles past Shoshone, signs begin cropping up, promoting the Ice Caves. LaRelle is still on Patrick's tail. *So, she's a local phenomenon! Has her own lore!* Amusing in a way—Claire would love her! Her brass. Except why does the local constabulary allow her to prowl? Why is it *his* job, dissuading her? It's going to cost time and money to detour into the Ice Caves. Can't the woman just be given a citation, some kind of warning to let her know she can't, at will, be predatory for her own amusement and gratification?

Baby, lighten up, Patrick can hear Claire chiding from the distance. *Give the lady some space.*

With the Ice Caves only a mile away, Patrick rolls down his window. LaRelle's still tailgating. Any braking and her pickup will be all over his rear. Patrick can hear her stereo blasting. He recognizes the voice but not the song—it's booming too much. He can see LaRelle laughing. Why?

He signals left, slows. She slows. He turns. She turns. Both into the Ice Caves' dirt drive. He sees her stop, sees the distance grow. *LaRelle really hates the Ice Caves*, Patrick can hear the officer. Okay, she's not leaving—but she's given up following.

Patrick pulls up to the concession shed, gets out, locks his Explorer, looks east down the road. LaRelle's Chevy's still there, engine obviously revving, because dust billows up lightly around its frame.

"How many?" the concession man, in coveralls and a red thermal shirt underneath, asks. He's been reading a book: *Sins of Nostradamus*. "How many?" he asks again.

"You see anyone else?" Patrick asks.

"What I've learned is, you never see everyone," the man says. He sticks his chin out.

"Okay, one then," Patrick says.

"One," the man repeats, and gives Patrick a ticket.

"Anyone else in there?" Patrick asks.

"Where?"

"The cave. The caves."

"People go in, people come out. I don't count," the man says.

When Patrick gets to the mouth, nobody stands to take a ticket. He waits. No one comes. He tries scanning east, to see whether LaRelle's still there. But he's come over a hump, and now he can't see. Finally, he starts walking. *Pay your fee, go inside, take the left passageway—smaller—she'll be outta your life,* Patrick hears the hunched sheriff informing his chili spoon.

Jesus: Ice is right! Patrick feels the chill at the mouth grip him, tighten, close in. The slate walls grow immediately slick, like black ice. The day, behind him, swallows itself. Patrick zips his blue polar shell to the neck, lets his eyes adjust. Along the cave wall stretches an orange extension cord—bare, low-wattage bulbs in wire baskets every hundred feet. Large as it promised to be, the cave has the feel of a grim anteroom. Some sort of cruel vault that, unlike the gentle body-hollows of desert sandstone, will never become the place hoped for, but always be the place endured before that place.

Patrick hears his own steps oddly amplified. They seem more accusation than mystery. *Take the left passageway.* How far in, down—the corridor shrinking then widening—will the second passageway be? And if LaRelle's afraid of caves, why go any further than the mouth? Just stay here? Wasn't fear *fear*? Courage *courage*? Love *love*? How did definitions get blurred?

Patrick thinks, *How did Claire draw me in in the first place? Away from Elaine?*

Patrick sees LaRelle waving Claire's letter tauntingly in the front seat of his Explorer, her fingers on Claire's words. It makes him cringe, as if Claire's tongue were somehow slipping incessantly between LaRelle's fingers.

He walks slowly, deliberately. Begins to count. Counts over eight hundred steps—when, indeed, a separate passageway, smaller, narrower, opens left, angling out of sight immediately, emanating a raw and grainy eminence.

Patrick enters and feels the darkness, behind, close like a door—an almost audible snap of lock sliding into casing. He can taste lime; his teeth, under his tongue, feel pumiced, pocked. *Far enough*, he thinks. *Good. Far enough.* Certainly, the idea isn't to go to the end, get lost. *Enough. Far enough. Enough distance. This is sufficient.*

Then, something out of the dark—a bat, probably—flies. Another. Another—flying so close Patrick swings around to keep whatever it is from his hair and jams his head into a blade of basalt which tears his cheek open. *Fuck!* he thinks, and brings his hand to his face, brings it away coated with blood. *Fuck!*

That's when he hears—and he knows the song—Vince Gill: "I Can't Tell You Why." Somebody approaching with a Walkman. Patrick can feel his face, sleek. Again, he looks at his hand—like snakeskin, red with one blink, green with the next. At once mineral and amphibian. Vince Gill's voice grows, amplifies, echoes. Then, thirty feet away, having made the bend, they appear, LaRelle and the man who seemed to be a sheriff. "Man follows instructions to a tee," the possible sheriff says. He carries a baseball bat.

"He does," LaRelle says. She lifts her earphones, turns off Vince Gill.

"Music off, it's quieter," the possible sheriff says.

"Fewer interruptions," LaRelle says.

"That seem reasonable?" the possible sheriff asks.

"Carter, look, he's bleeding," LaRelle says.

"Jesus, the man can't even walk into a cave!" The possible sheriff, Carter, seems annoyed. "Let's get a look at—"

"I mean it: keep your hands off me," Patrick says. He backs away.

"He's done EMT," LaRelle says. "Carter here, my man. He knows CPR."

"Right. EMT, CPR. I'm sure!" Patrick snaps. "So the idea's

to beat the shit out of me?" He flares his eyes, grinds his teeth.

"Hey! We never—"

"Take my Explorer? Head off into the sunset?" He's seen a dozen TV episodes like this. *Creepy assholes!* He's read the tabloids.

"Wait! You talking about auto theft? Maybe grand—?"

"Carter, what's the sentence on that?" LaRelle asks. "Grand auto—whatever."

"Hey, it's high."

"High. I thought."

"Why do I think you may not be who you're dressed as?" Patrick says to Carter.

"Don't know, give up. You're a skeptic?"

"Hey, traveler—hey. All we are, here, is our bodies," LaRelle says.

"And our voices," Carter adds. "And our hearts."

"Bodies and voices—up close and personal. The rest is dust," LaRelle says.

"Steam. Hereafter."

The two, in their throats, make a kind of low, timbrous music, an emission Patrick judges to be laughter.

"Fine, okay, tell me what you want," Patrick says.

"What we want is simple," Carter says. "Lean in. Pay attention. Hear our story."

Patrick tries focusing them but can only frame them one at a time. He feels blood seeping, crusting his cheek. The cut's deep. Something, though, about the moment is weirdly pleasurable.

"Hear our story," the possible sheriff repeats.

"Hear your story?" Patrick's confused.

"It's a love story," LaRelle says.

"Except no one will listen," Carter says. He swings the bat he carries into the dank, limestone air. "Assholes!" he screams.

Patrick recoils, throws his hands out—the back of his left hand hits a jag on the cave wall. "Christ!" Patrick says. "Fuck!"

"We begin our story, and people drive off," LaRelle says.

"People can't take it. They say it's a too-close-for-comfort love story. And they get up and walk away," Carter says.

He whips the air again—Patrick, this time, trying to hold his ground.

"Careful," Carter says, nodding toward the blood mixing now between Patrick's fingers. "This cave's a potato peeler. They say, one time, man came in—all alone like you—somehow worked himself up into a panic, running to get out, bouncing off the walls. Peeled himself to death. Person loses control, his insides can become his outsides."

"Whose words are these?" LaRelle asks Patrick point blank, her voice honed with a ferocity.

What's she asking? What's she getting at?

But then she begins quoting: "*I want us to be in a world where we don't have to stop. I want us to be on an island circled by tiger sharks, handcuffed to each other on a bed made up of raw oysters and ice so that neither of us can tell the difference between the sex we make and the sex we eat, between hypothermia and hunger.* Who? Whose words?"

It is, of course, Claire, her letter. Patrick doesn't answer.

"*Claire.* They're your friend—she still your friend?—your friend Claire's words. I'm a quick study when it comes to love. And Claire's words burned me, so I memorized them. So—what's your name?" LaRelle asks. "Mr. Ford Explorer. I want your name. What's the name you go by? Besides, I mean, Baby—she wrote Baby, which you're obviously not. You got any antiseptic, Carter?"

"Just our Wild Turkey," Carter says. "Answer the lady. What's your name?"

"Patrick," Patrick says.

"Patrick."

"Patrick."

"What's your evaluation of love, Patrick?" Carter asks.

Patrick tries measuring, weighing the moment: how crazy

the two might be, what they intend. Is his being left dead here, in the rock and ice, inevitable?

"Given what LaRelle's said about your letter, I would imagine you'd have some sort of major and cogent evaluation of—"

"Love? Hey, *everybody* has some sort of evaluation!" Patrick feels impatient.

"And yours is?"

"Would you like me to quote again?" LaRelle grins.

"You know the heat of love?" Carter asks. "The ignition point?"

"I know what the heat *does*," Patrick says. He wipes the blood from the back of his left hand across his face. His blood smells like the cave.

"And do you like that? What the heat of love does?"

"And is it good? For you? That feeling," LaRelle asks.

"Why don't we change the subject," Patrick says.

"*We* like it," Carter says. "Love's flash-point. The heat of love. Love's heat."

"Very much," LaRelle says.

"It's just—" LaRelle searches the web of her open fingers.

Carter finishes her sentence. "It's just, the people we're married to: *they* don't like it."

"No."

"No. Not at—"

"*All*."

"They make judgments. Superior judgments."

"They don't understand," LaRelle says.

"Can we tell you our story?" Carter asks.

The passage of the ice cave—perhaps the whole cave—seems to shift. *What is an ice cave, anyway?* Patrick has a notion or memory, something he'd read, been told, that it's where early settlers hacked frozen blocks, carried them to wagons, drove them home, refrigerated. *Why am I hot? It should be cooler here.*

"Will you listen?" Carter asks.

"We'd be grateful," LaRelle says.

"I have this sense that it's not really a choice," Patrick says.

"Hey—*everything!*" Carter swings his bat, this time listlessly. Still, Patrick sidesteps. "*Everything's* a choice, man! Don't you think?"

"Are you a sheriff?" Patrick asks. "For the record?"

"*For* the record—*with* the record," Carter announces. "Deputy." He grins.

"Three times a week," LaRelle offers.

"Three days I get to drive the car," he says.

"So, Patrick Baby," LaRelle pauses.

"Leave it alone," Patrick says.

"Did you think I meant you? Before? Doing the nasty? Back wherever—the truck stop. Listen, no offense but you're not who I'd leave footprints on the windshield for. And it's a done thing anyway. Carter and I. Your Explorer. Footprints. They're there." She laughs. "And some other…stains."

Carter laughs, throws his head back. "Use all the freshener you want—you'll still smell us. For a week!" he says.

Patrick feels something churn in his chest, belly, slide—some kind of dislocation of regret, memory, anger, longing. He remembers a chair. A balcony. A broken wine glass. Coconut cream pie. A floor. A fire. Pillows.

"Love is insane," Carter says.

"It's too much for this world," LaRelle says.

"World can't hold it."

"A-men!"

"Hey. I burned my house down. Burned my family out of a place to live because of love," Carter says. With a sudden flail of his bat, he dislodges a stalactite, which falls by Patrick's feet and shatters. "Love is insane," Carter announces.

"Let us tell you our story," LaRelle almost pleads.

They unsheathe a story of randomness. A story of being accidentally in the same place and knowing immediately. Then trying to move away. Attempting to get out of the radius. Out of the hot, crazed, metal-bending circle and its knowing heat. Trying but not trying to adjust torque. Right the too-loose drift. Preferring the prickles of skin, the raised short hair. The sense their eyelids were flash paper. That they could lift a lethal knife and plunge it for the sake of just a moment, pull the trigger of any offered gun. That they might/did/would cross boundaries, break laws, ruin lives in order to—however they might—throw back another glass of randomness, empty the plate of accident and be hungry again.

"It was like all of the burning rollovers I've ever pulled people out of, at once," Carter says.

"It was like killing my children," LaRelle says, "and being glad."

"Not that she did," Carter adds.

"Right. Not that I didn't, too," LaRelle says.

"It's been like—you see the movie Fargo? It's been like feeding most of the rest of the world into a tree-eater."

"Amazing!" LaRelle says.

"Demented!"

"Deranged!"

"The sex you have is a cannibal."

"But you can't stop."

"Eating it."

"Having it eat you."

"Even though you try and try and try!"

"So, Patrick, you say you've known that?" Carter asks.

Patrick is hyperventilating, blood rushing to and from his face, his hand, seeping out. It feels like snot. It feels like motor oil. And what has happened to the ice? The cave steams, it seems. Patrick imagines the three of them are in the backdraft of a house fire. "Maybe this is where you tell me why I'm here," he says. "Why you've abducted me."

"Whoa! Whoa, Baby, whoa!"

"Whoa!" Carter echoes.

"You don't get it?" LaRelle grills.

"I don't think I—"

"He say *abducted*?" Carter asks. "He use the word—?"

"He did. Abducted. Someone had to hear us," LaRelle makes clear.

"Do you know what it's like, no one listening?" Carter asks.

"Are you—? You couldn't be! Are you saying—telling us that you never answered that letter from the ice-and-oysters lady—whatshername?" LaRelle asks.

"Claire," Patrick says.

"Clean those cuts up," Carter demands. "Bleeding's not a bad thing; it can be a good thing. Still—comes a point, you have to clean the bleeding up."

The three stand. Wait. For what? Something—in the cave with its walls like teeth, like ice, glistening. The cave hovers and encases them; light, such as it is, contracting then relaxing. It seems all the telling is over, and whatever the next thing is awaits—a moment, a tentative move, an uncertain question.

"So, anyway—thanks," Carter says. "Here's half a bottle of Wild Turkey. For hearing us. Wash those cuts."

"You never know," LaRelle says.

"You start down a road—"

"Road not on the map—"

"Anything's possible."

"People arrive—"

"People depart—"

"It's a fucking airport," LaRelle says.

Carter swings his bat into the wall. Shards, cave fragments, crystals fly, sound, crumble, echo. "Stuff builds up," he says. "No matter how hard you try—fucking stuff builds up."

"He's just a deputy sheriff, but he's a wise man," LaRelle says.

With that, the two—sheriff and sheriff's lover—turn and trail a wake of departure, distance, rounding a corner of the passage, Vince Gill faintly playing again, "Never Knew Lonely."

Eyes closed, Patrick tries to sense his placement: a compass point, the sky, a shore. Nothing rights itself, though, and he feels remote, equidistant from what, any other time, he might have designated *highway* or *December, Apalachicola* or *next week*. Blind, all he can recognize is the slow pump of his heart, steadily squeezing blood. He's a man with no sense of direction who is bleeding and beginning to shake, feeling his mouth fill up with mucous and with salt, his own eccentric tide.

He begins walking, eyes still shut—partly to test, partly to let the folly of himself take full reign. He can feel his weight, of a sudden, slide in what is not quite mud, tip, correct, break something off (icicle? limestone?) overhead *Am I going in or out? Toward or away? Is this—how does one know?—new territory? Or am I walking in circles? Am I—what's, even, the question I'm asking? Does it matter?*

When Patrick lets his lids finally rise, it's more the idea of seeing than seeing which he rejoins—as if, at first, actual sight hasn't found its circuitry. It is still—for a second or two or three—the dull, dark inside of his brain. He is, it seems, moving only on the inside of his skull—mapless and anesthetized, where no one thing speaks of any other thing in this world. He's the salt, he's the mucous coating his mouth, dumbly, the mere tar bog of his melted mind. If there are orange electrical cord bulbs in baskets along the ice cave wall, they are all out. Or he has walked past them, perhaps. Or someone on the outside has thrown a switch.

When he emerges, his Explorer is intact. The day has warmed slightly, seems more open to light. High desert fields of lava rock spread out: their own black and vermillion version of a meadow. Patrick stands, fingers on the handle of the door, the door not quite cracked. He isn't sure he wants what he'll find inside. Confirmation that it has been occupied, been used—LaRelle and Carter, indelible in its atmosphere.

But, finally, he opens the door. And they have been there. Together. They have spoken the truth, and the truth, their truth, is as heady as sludge, all the musk of mother-of-pearl—sweet as meringue, caked like salt.

Patrick climbs inside. Shuts the door. Leaves the windows tight. An hour later, clothes still on, Patrick sits like a child in the slow riffles of the Big Wood River, listening to the scribble of the water, lifting stones. It's hard to breath. Something in him feels scourged. Something else feels suffocated, drowning. *Idaho*, he thinks. And then, *Idaho...Idaho.*

ABOUT THE AUTHOR

David Kranes is a playwright and author of two volumes of short stories and seven novels. His 2001 novel, *The National Tree*, was adapted for television and aired on the Hallmark channel in November 2009. His short fiction has won literary prizes and has appeared in such magazines as *Esquire, Ploughshares*, and *Transatlantic Review*. Over fifty of his plays have been performed in New York and across the U.S., and his radio plays have been performed in the U.S., Canada, and abroad. The opera *Orpheus Lex*, for which Mr. Kranes wrote the libretto, was performed at New York City's Symphony Space in February 2010. His volume of selected plays was published in August of 2011. A new play, *The Last Word*, developed at NYC's Lark Theater, was recently given a staged reading at Salt Lake Acting Company. In his second (or is it third?) life, Mr. Kranes travels and consults the casino industry.

ABOUT TORREY HOUSE PRESS

The economy is a wholly owned subsidiary of the environment, not the other way around.
—*Senator Gaylord Nelson, founder of Earth Day*

Headquartered in Salt Lake City and Torrey, Utah, Torrey House Press is an independent book publisher of literary fiction and creative nonfiction about the environment, people, cultures, and resource management issues relating to America's wild places. Torrey House Press endeavors to increase awareness of and appreciation for the importance of natural landscape through the power of pen and story.

2% for the West is a trademark of Torrey House Press designating that two percent of Torrey House Press sales are donated to a select group of not-for-profit environmental organizations and used to create a scholarship available to up-and-coming writers at college environmental humanities programs.

Torrey House Press
www.torreyhouse.com

See www.torreyhouse.com for our thought-provoking *The Legend's Daughter* Discussion Guide.

ALSO AVAILABLE FROM TORREY HOUSE PRESS

The Ordinary Truth by Jana Richman

When Nell Jorgensen buried her husband after a hunting accident, she buried a piece of herself, her relationship with her daughter, and more than one secret along with him. Now, thirty-six years later, her granddaughter Cassie intends to unearth those secrets and repair those relationships, but she's unprepared for what she finds. Set in the sparse and beautiful landscape of Nevada's Spring Valley and Schell Creek Mountains, award-winning author Jana Richman brings us an emotional journey of love, loss, and family steeped in the realities of the colliding urban and rural worlds of the West.

Recapture by Erica Olsen

The stories in *Recapture* take us to an American West that is both strange and familiar. The Grand Canyon can only be visited in replica form. An archivist preserves a rare map of a vanished Lake Tahoe. A Utah cliff dwelling survives as an aging roadside attraction in California. By turns lyrical, deadpan, and surreal, Erica Olsen's stories bring us the natural world and the world we make, the artifacts we keep and the memories and desires that shape our lives.

Tributary by Barbara K. Richardson

Willa Cather and Sandra Dallas resonate in Richardson's fearless portrait of 1870s Mormon Utah. This smart and lively novel tracks the extraordinary life of one woman who dares resist communal salvation in order to find her own. Clair Martin's dauntless search for self leads her from the domination of Mormon polygamy to the chaos of Reconstruction Dixie and back to Utah.

The Scholar of Moab by Steven L. Peck

A mysterious redactor finds the journals of Hyrum Thayne, a high school dropout and wannabe scholar, who manages to wreak havoc among townspeople who are convinced he can save them from a band of mythic Book of Mormon thugs and Communists. Peck's hilarious novel considers questions of consciousness and contingency, and the very way humans structure meaning.

Grind by Mark Maynard

Gritty and irreverent, eight linked stories set near Reno, Nevada, bring a colorful band of characters to vivid life. These stories play out within sight of the Mother Lode hotel and casino, a glass monolith that looms over downtown Reno and whose peeling façade represents the city's dwindling past and the uncertain future.

Crooked Creek by Maximilian Werner

Sara and Preston, along with Sara's little brother Jasper, must flee Arizona when Sara's family runs afoul of American Indian artifact hunters. Evoking the lyricism of Cormac McCarthy and the elegance of Wallace Stegner, Werner combines vivid characters with brilliant tension in this potent allegory set in the nineteenth century West.

The Plume Hunter by Renée Thompson

When Fin McFaddin takes to plume hunting—killing birds to collect feathers for women's hats—to support his widowed mother, he finds danger, controversy, and heartache amid the marshes of nineteenth century Oregon. In 1885, hunters like Fin killed more than five million birds in the United States for the millinery industry, prompting the formation of the Audubon Society.

Printed in the USA
CPSIA information can be obtained
at www.ICGtesting.com
JSHW022344140824
68134JS00019B/1670